❤ ❤ ❤ ❤ ❤ ❤ ❤ ❤ ❤ ❤ ❤ ❤ ❤ ❤ ❤ ❤ ❤

Dear Mom,

I just knew you and Adam would be perfect for each other. He's really nice...and the fact that he's also very good-looking doesn't exactly hurt, either! So why isn't anything happening with you two? I know you've turned avoiding people into, like, an art form. But Adam doesn't seem to be taking the hint, and sometimes I think you really like him....

So really, Mom, what's stopping you? I say go for it!

Your loving daughter,

Sydney

Please address questions and book requests to: Silhouette Reader Service
U.S.: 3010 Walden Ave., P.O. Box 1325, Buffalo, NY 14269
Canadian: P.O. Box 609, Fort Erie, Ont. L2A 5X3

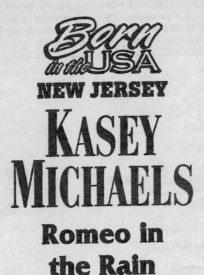

Born in the USA

NEW JERSEY

KASEY MICHAELS

Romeo in the Rain

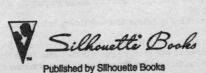

Silhouette Books

Published by Silhouette Books
America's Publisher of Contemporary Romance

SILHOUETTE BOOKS
300 East 42nd St.,
New York, N.Y. 10017

RECYCLED PAPER

ISBN 0-373-47180-7

ROMEO IN THE RAIN

Dear Reader,

To Manhattan dweller Courtney Blackmun, the best thing about New Jersey was its view of New York. But that was before she traveled to the state and fell in love with Ocean City, which just happens to be one of my own favorite places on earth.

Every year our family leaves Pennsylvania and goes "down the shore" to Ocean City, to walk the sandy beaches, to "eat" our way down the boardwalk, to watch the sun rise over the Atlantic Ocean. And nearly every year I arrive back home with another idea for a story set in this most magical place.

Bruce Springsteen, who wrote the song "Born in the U.S.A.," happens to hail from New Jersey, which makes me believe the title of this special Silhouette series is particularly suited to *Romeo in the Rain* and Courtney's growing love affair with the state. My own "love affair" with New Jersey's shore continued after *Romeo in the Rain*, to include two more previously published Silhouette Romance novels, *Sydney's Folly* and *Timely Matrimony*.

What can I say? I just flat-out have fallen in love with New Jersey. I hope, dear reader, that you do, too!

To Ocean City, New Jersey,
for being the perfect spot for lovers to find both
themselves and each other;
to Sue Charles, for finding me the perfect condo
on the perfect beach.

Chapter One

"It can't be! Courtney, darling? Is that really you? Why, it *is* you. Imagine that—Courtney Blackmun in the *library*, just as if she was an ordinary mortal. I would have thought a famous writer could order books delivered—you know, like pizza?"

Pulling the pair of oversize horn-rimmed glasses slightly away from her highly recognizable emerald-green eyes, Courtney raised her makeup-free face to see her friend Suzi Harper—head reviewer of *Literary Lines*, a national book-review magazine—staring down at her in openmouthed amazement.

"Well, I'm stumped, Suzi. How did you see through my disguise? I thought I was undetectable. Jeans and a scrungy sweatshirt have always worked before—that and this ponytail." She gave her head a slight shake, sending the long ebony ponytail twitching. "Just what gave me away?" she asked, keeping her voice low.

Suzi subsided into a facing chair, her ruby-tipped hands gripping the scarred wooden table top as if she were physically keeping her petite size-five body from slipping to the floor in a faint. "Good Lord, it *is* you! Courtney! I don't believe it! What happened—were you robbed? I mean, you aren't even wearing *mascara!* Where's the Courtney Blackmun whose gorgeous, smiling face was just splashed all over the cover of *Literary Lines*' major competitor's spring preview issue?"

Courtney closed the reference book she had been paging through aimlessly before the interruption, laid it on top of a stack of similar books and pushed the whole lot of them to one side. "That was my evil twin on the cover, Suzi. The real Courtney hates mascara, you know that. And do you think you can keep it down? New York City is a great place to hide, and I like my anonymity. I don't want anyone to know I'm here."

As Suzi opened her mouth to protest, Courtney went on hurriedly, "So, how's it going? And, while we're at it—what are you doing here? You must have to read a dozen new books a week, without coming in here to find more."

"Two dozen, and no, I'm not here to read. I just had an inspiration and popped in to check the source on a quote I want to use in a review. Hey—maybe you'll know. After all, you're a writer."

"I don't know, Suzi," Courtney said, laughing weakly. "Not every reviewer has been as kind to me over the years as you've always been."

Suzi waved one hand, dismissing any opinion but her own. "You aren't just a writer—you're a *great* writer. Always have been, always will be. Now, with that out of the way, maybe you can help me. The librarian just pointed me in this direction, as if I'd know what to do next. You wouldn't happen to know who said— Wait a minute, I have it written down in here somewhere."

Courtney watched as Suzi dug into the bottom of her Gucci bag, fighting the urge to run—while the running was still good—because Suzi's blithely tossed compliment had nearly reduced Courtney to tears.

"*Voilà!* Here it is!" Suzi exclaimed, pulling a small crumpled notebook from the purse and holding it up as if she had just discovered gold.

"Ssh!" hissed a middle-aged man at the next table. "Some people, young lady, come to the library to read."

Suzi shook her head. "I don't know, Courtney," she remarked, lowering her voice. "At times like this I wonder where chivalry has gone. He didn't even say please."

Courtney wearily rubbed her forehead. She had come here hoping to jog something loose by reading random nonfiction accounts of the Old West, but it wasn't working. She hadn't had an original idea since entering the library—only the growing conviction that she was wasting her time. All she wanted to do now was crawl away somewhere and have a cup of coffee and a cigarette. "The quote, Suzi," she prompted quietly.

"Oh, right. Here it is. 'Sweet is revenge—especially to women.' Great, huh? I saw it on a T-shirt on Seventh Avenue and I want to use it in my review about— Well, that doesn't matter. Suffice it to say that a certain well-known actor is soon going to be very sorry he wasn't kinder to his ex-wife. You would have thought she would have been happy with the villa in Cannes. I know *I* would have. But not her. Oh, no. Boy, talk about your poison-pen 'tell all' books. I mean, this woman really raked that guy over the—"

"Byron. George Noel Gordon—Lord Byron," Courtney answered shortly, smiling wryly as she watched the middle-aged man rise and head for the reference librarian's desk, most probably to demand that Suzi Harper and her grubby-looking companion be thrown out of the library—and their library cards fed into a paper shredder. "It's from *Don Juan,* canto one, if memory serves. And now I suggest we get out of here before we're asked to leave." She picked up the books she had been working with and placed them on a Return Here cart. "Are you hungry, Suzi?"

Ten minutes later, as they were seated at a booth in a small, nearly deserted sandwich shop with two cups of steaming coffee in front of them, Suzi remarked, "Fifteen books—and all bestsellers! I wish I could have reviewed all of them—not that I haven't read them all, of course. I don't know how you do it."

"Fourteen books—thirteen of them bestsellers—but who's counting," Courtney corrected facetiously, picking up her cup. "But remember, Suzi, a writer is only as good as her next book. So, are you going to give me the name of this Hollywood actor whose ex just rained all over his parade, or am I going to have to wait for next week's copy of *Literary Lines*?''

The reviewer, her eyes narrowing speculatively as she leaned across the table at Courtney, replied softly, ''Only if you promise to tell me what you were doing in the library. Research for your new book? I know the one that's coming out in the spring is set in Russia during the time of the czars. What is it this time? Fourteenth-century England? The French Revolution? The Civil Wa-*ar*? Come on, Courtney—give!''

Courtney reached into her purse, extracted a lighter and an unopened pack of cigarettes, then replaced both items without opening the pack. Suzi was getting too close. ''There's nothing to tell, Suzi. I was merely passing time. I was just about to leave because I wanted to have a cigarette.''

''But we've been sitting in the smoking section for nearly fifteen minutes and you haven't lit up yet,'' Suzi pointed out rationally, still staring at Courtney in a way that had Courtney wishing she had not given in to the impulse to seek inspiration at the library. ''You didn't even open the pack.''

Courtney snapped her purse closed and set it back down on the floor. ''No, of course I didn't. I just said I had *wanted* a cigarette. Smoking will kill you. Everybody knows that, which is why I quit. I only smoke when I'm writing—and at times like this.''

Now why had she added that? Courtney wished it were humanly possible to sit in a too-tight café booth and kick herself at the same time. All she could do was hope that Suzi hadn't picked up on her verbal slip.

Courtney wasn't going to be that lucky. "A time like this?" the reviewer asked, putting down her cup. "And what kind of time *is* this, darling? I didn't want to mention it, friend, but frankly—you look like hell."

Now she had done it. She had opened the door to her private life and Suzi would be like a dog with a bone until she got some answers. But maybe that was why Courtney had allowed that verbal slip. Maybe she wanted to talk about it—*had* to talk about it—and Suzi was as good an audience as any other she could think of at the moment.

Courtney closed her eyes, a very real pain clutching at her gut. "I'm blocked." The admission was a whisper, barely audible.

Suzi leaned forward avidly, her body so taut it appeared to quiver. "You're *what*?"

Courtney spoke from between clenched teeth. "You heard me. Stop waving those antennae around before you draw a crowd. I'm *blocked*, damn it!" she gritted. "Completely, totally, one hundred and ten percent blocked! I wasn't in the library doing research. I was searching for help—some inspiration, *anything!* I haven't written a word in six months."

Sitting back against the hard wooden booth, Suzi stared at the writer who had published fourteen books in ten years. It seemed impossible. It was easy to see from Suzi's expression that she would have found it easier to believe that Niagara Falls had been stopped up with a ten-cent cork. "You're kidding," she said, looking hard at the dark sunglasses Courtney had donned when they'd left the library.

Courtney took in a deep breath and let it out on a sigh. Yes, this was good. She almost felt as if she had just been to confession. Admitting her problem, the problem she had hidden from her agent, her publisher, and most especially her daughter, had actually begun to ease the terrible tension that had been holding her chest tight in its grip.

"Would I kid you about a thing like that?" Courtney quipped, grinning at Suzi, although the smile was forced and couldn't last. "Even smoking doesn't help, which is why I put the pack away. God, Suzi, I can't tell you how awful this is. I know this is going to sound trite, and maybe being blocked is making me think in clichés, but I feel as if a large part of me has died. My brain, probably."

The reviewer waved her manicured hands as if calling for a time-out. "Now wait a minute, Courtney. Your brain isn't dead—you're just temporarily burned-out, stressed-out. It happens. There have been hundreds of articles and books written about writer's block. I should know—I've had to review half a dozen of them myself. Have you tried reading some of them for help? I could recommend a couple of—"

Courtney nodded, cutting off her friend. "I've read them all—twice—and no, they haven't helped. You know, Suzi," she said, "I always thought writer's block was a joke, or a cop-out used by writers who were just plain lazy. You know how it is. There are all those sayings about writing. Like, you just stare at the blank page until drops of blood show up on your forehead. Or, writing is the loneliest profession in the world. Or the one about hating to write but loving having written. I never believed them. To me, writing is—was—a joy. Well, let me tell you—those sayings are all true. In spades!''

"That tough, huh?'' Suzi asked, biting her bottom lip. "And you haven't written *anything?*''

Courtney shook her head. "Nothing. Zilch. Nada. Oh, I've *written*—but it's all garbage, not worth saving.'' Her voice lowered and she heard an unwanted tremble steal into her tone. "I'm scared, Suzi. Writing isn't just what I do—it's what I am. I feel like a composer who has suddenly gone tone deaf—or an artist who's been struck blind. It's all gone. What if I can't do it anymore, Suzi? What if I'm never able to do it again? Courtney Blackmun will cease to exist!'' She stopped talking and hung her head, tears stinging her eyes. "Oh, damn! I didn't mean to cry on your shoulder. I'm sorry, Suzi.''

Suzi patted Courtney's hand sympathetically. "Hey, what are friends for if you can't cry all over them? Don't give it another thought. Does Wilbur know about your block?''

"My publisher? No. Nobody knows. Except you,'' Courtney amended, slipping the sunglasses down to the end of her nose so that she could use her napkin to wipe at her eyes. What was wrong with her? She *never* cried. She had said too much and knew it was time to rein in her emotions before she broke down completely. "Why did you ask about Wilbur?'' she questioned, hoping she was up to a feeble joke. "Should I have kept my big mouth shut? Are you going to blackmail me now, Suzi-Q?"

"Moi?" her friend exclaimed, her eyes wide. "Nonsense, darling. I'm going to help you. But don't believe I'm doing it merely out of the kindness of my heart. I have to read too many bad books to consider the possibility of never having another Courtney Blackmun masterpiece to enjoy. Now, listen to me. I have the greatest idea."

Courtney shook her head, smiling. "You don't know how I've learned to dread those words from you, Suzi. The last time you had the *greatest idea* we ended up suffering through that off-off-Broadway show that had all the cast members wearing paper bags over their heads. I couldn't understand a word they said—which may have been the only good thing to happen the whole night."

Suzi pulled a face. "Boy, oh boy. Make one eensy-weensy little mistake, and nobody ever forgets it. But not this time—honest! Now listen to me, Courtney. Remember that crack I made about a villa in Cannes? Well, I may not have one of those, but I do have a great little condo in Ocean City that I inherited from my great-uncle Charlie, bless his soul. It's November, so the tourists have all gone home. The place is yours for as long as you need to stay. It's quiet, *secluded,* smack-dab on the ocean—the perfect place to work your way through this temporary block. And it is temporary, I'm sure of it."

Courtney closed her eyes, considering Suzi's offer.

It sounded tempting. A little solitude might be just what she needed. Besides, at least one of the articles she'd read on writer's block mentioned the benefits of a change of scenery. "Ocean City? Where's Ocean City? No, no, don't tell me. I can see it already. It's tucked somewhere along the beautiful brooding coastline of Cape Cod."

Suzi laughed, dismissing Cape Cod as second-rate. "Good heavens, no. Ocean City is in New Jersey, only eight or so miles south of Atlantic City and all those lovely casinos. But Ocean City is quiet. This time of year it must be absolutely tomblike! It's even a dry town—you know, no liquor sold within the city limits. It's advertised as a family-resort town."

"New Jersey!" Courtney blurted, causing the waitress to look at her curiously. Courtney was a New Yorker, born and bred, and had a true New Yorker's disdain for New Jersey. To her mind, the only thing good about New Jersey was its view of Manhattan. "You've got to be kidding! For crying out loud, Suzi, I'm not *that* hard up!"

"Aren't you, darling?" Suzi Harper purred, batting her long, mascara-tipped eyelashes. "Far be it from me to act as judge, but then I'm not the one who was hiding out in the public library—or blubbering in a coffee shop."

"I'll think about it," Courtney promised weakly, motioning to the waitress to bring them menus, for she had suddenly realized that she was hungry. "New Jersey! Good God, has it really come to that?"

* * *

Adam Richardson walked slowly along the deserted beach, his hands stuffed deep in the pockets of a pair of tan cord slacks rolled up to his knees, the back and hood of his unzipped white nylon windbreaker billowing behind him as the ocean breeze caught them like sails heading into the wind.

His thick black hair, grown just a little too long, swept across his tanned forehead and tumbled over the lenses of his dark sunglasses, so that now and then he gave a slight toss of his head in a halfhearted attempt to rearrange the tousled locks.

He was barefoot, even though the wet sand was cold against the soles of his feet. Adam liked the feeling. He liked the feel of the wind against his face. He liked the quiet of his surroundings, a silence broken only by the occasional cry of a sea gull in search of a tasty lunch, circling the seemingly endless strip of sand that divided resort town and ocean.

More than anything else, Adam Richardson liked the freedom he felt, the peace, the solitude, and the total absence of the necessity to do anything more basic than breathe.

He had been running for so long—forever. It was difficult to believe that anything was real any more—that anyone was real. Even himself. As he had told Beatrice just two nights ago, he had begun to think his face had been permanently frozen into what the press called his winning smile.

Beatrice. Adam smiled, but this smile felt good, natural. *God love Beatrice*. It had been her idea that he come here, to the beach, to a place where he could be alone, to unwind and recover the stamina that all the months of running, of planning, of back-room maneuvering and public debate had drained from him.

He stopped walking to push his sunglasses up onto his head. He *was* real—or at least he hoped he was. How difficult it still was, after being surrounded by adoring hordes whose acclamation he'd hoped he'd learned to live with if not totally disbelieve, to try to remember Adam Richardson, *man*—and not merely Adam Richardson, *packaged product*.

He turned around, to head back to the condo.

There were storm clouds coming up from the south; Adam could see them in the distance. Even though the November sun was still warm, there would be rain and a steep drop in temperature by morning, he was sure of it, especially since he had already heard the local weather report forecast heavy rain for the next four days.

Adam smiled. He had walked the beach in the sun. Soon he would know what it was like to walk that same beach in the rain.

"Good Lord, I still don't believe I let Suzi talk me into this."

The windshield wipers beat back and forth against the curved tinted glass in tune with the sixties rock-and-roll song on the radio as Courtney squinted to see through the cold November rain. So this was Ocean City, *New Jersey.*

It looked like a ghost town.

Ever since entering the island town by way of the

Ninth Street Causeway—stopping only to grab a quick lunch at the fast-food restaurant whose golden arches had called to her from out of the gray mist—Courtney had been driving aimlessly through the streets, hopelessly lost.

The map tossed carelessly on the passenger seat of her Mercedes was less than useless, considering that it had been Suzi Harper's own creation. It listed beauty parlors, restaurants, movie houses, "adorable" boutiques, and a single X that supposedly marked the location of her condo.

What it didn't do was show Courtney that the city's streets were designed around the curve of the shoreline and had a maddening tendency to turn into dead ends.

Courtney would have stopped to ask directions if she could have brought herself to believe there was a single soul alive in the entire town. She knew there had to be year-round residents, but they were obviously an intelligent bunch and knew when to come in out of the rain. If only she could remember how to get back to the restaurant—surely someone there would be able to help her!

Then she saw a sign on the next corner, the wind off the ocean buffeting the slim metal marker so that it appeared to be waving, beckoning to her. Wesley Avenue. She put on her right turn signal, mentally chiding herself for the action, which would be seen only by the sea gulls, and slowly headed south, straining to see house numbers on the large sprawling assortment of condos and private homes.

Just as the road seemed about to disappear into a heavy wet sand dune, she found it.

Courtney turned the Mercedes left into the wide concrete driveway and turned off the engine, leaning back against the soft burgundy leather seat and sighing in exhaustion as she looked down at her watch.

Two o'clock. Had she really set out from Manhattan before ten in the morning? This *same* morning? She felt exhausted, as if she had just driven across the entire country.

As the heavy rain sheeted down the windshield, she looked out at the two-story gray-shingle building that housed Suzi's condo and one other. Suzi's unit was on the left, her friend had told her, and Courtney peered to the right to see a second door that led into the other condo. There were no lights burning in either unit, not that Courtney had expected the other side of the condo to be inhabited. Surely there couldn't be two people crazy enough to vacation in Ocean City in November!

Courtney allowed herself a small smile. She had to admit the place looked good so far, and she could hear the pounding of the surf nearby, now that the car radio was silent.

Yes, maybe it was possible. Maybe she *could* work here.

She continued to look around, trying to summon up the nerve to step out into the driving rain, and her stomach tightened into a warning knot. She sensed that something was wrong. But what was it?

"A car?" she whispered at last, as if the low-slung

cherry-red sports car parked beside the Mercedes had
ears. "How can there be a car?" She looked toward
the dark windows of the condo on her right once more.
"It couldn't be. I'm supposed to be here alone."

Courtney's right hand automatically reached toward
the ignition. No way. No, sir. No way, no how! Suzi
wasn't pulling any of her little tricks on her! She had
told her friend she needed inspiration. She should have
known. To Suzi, inspiration was a first-choice syno-
nym for a *man*. She had probably imported a long-lost
cousin or something to liven up Courtney's life.
"Well, thanks, but no thanks, Suzi old chum!" she
said decisively. "I'm outta here!"

Just as she was about to turn the key, there was a
knock at the window beside her. Quickly depressing
the button that locked all four doors, she turned her
head slightly, then slid her eyes to the left—just like
one of the three little pigs, she thought hysterically—
to see who was knock, knock, knocking at her door.

The two-legged wolf, or cousin, wore a bright yellow slicker, its oversize hood falling forward over his
face as he bent his body almost in half to peer in at
her.

Tall, her brain registered randomly. Tall, and dark.
He was smiling at her, a wide, open welcoming smile.

And with very white teeth, Courtney added silently,
staring at his mouth in spite of herself. At least Suzi's
cousin had had the benefit of first-rate orthodontics.

He was making some sort of circular motion with
his hand, she noted vaguely as her attention was
caught and held by his long, peculiarly slanted eyes,

eyes as gray as the day but holding none of the storminess she would have expected.

Courtney shivered, although she wasn't cold. *And he'll huff and he'll puff, and he'll—*

"What?" she called to him, wrinkling her forehead. "Oh! I get it now. You want me to open my window." She shook her head, slowly, for emphasis. "Not by the hair on my chinny-chin-chin, buster," she called through the glass. "You can tell Suzi she struck out with this one. *Now* what is he doing?"

The man had straightened and moved to the front of the Mercedes, a tall, yellow barrier between Courtney and the door to the condo. He was gesturing, first to the door on her right, then to himself, then to the door on the left—her door.

And he was still smiling.

"Oh, God," Courtney groaned. "He's not supposed to be my accidental roommate. It's even worse than that. He's going to be my neighbor! What are the odds on having a neighbor in an Ocean City condo in November? A thousand to one? A *million* to one? How did I ever get so lucky? Don't I have enough problems? He's probably desperate for company and won't leave me alone for a minute."

Unable to believe the situation could get any worse and not caring for the idea of heading back to Manhattan just in time for rush-hour traffic, Courtney made a decision. She might have to be a neighbor, but she didn't have to be a *good* neighbor. She wasn't an ambassador to a foreign country—she was a woman.

"A woman who can—as her own daughter has informed her on more than one occasion—do a great imitation of a dragon with a lousy disposition,'' she murmured, reaching for her purse and the key to the condo before throwing open the door of the Mercedes and stepping onto the driveway. "So let's go breathe some fire, woman!'' she muttered quietly to herself in encouragement.

"Hi, there!'' the tall dark man with the very white teeth called, advancing on her with his right hand held out in greeting. "Unless you're lost, it looks like we're going to be neighbors. It's good to see you. I was beginning to feel like the only living soul left in the world. I'm Adam, by the way. Adam Richardson.''

Courtney looked pointedly at the outstretched hand, then up at Adam's smiling face, her own expression carefully deadpan. She had been right the second time—he wasn't Suzi's cousin, but he was desperate for company. The smartest thing she could do would be to get rid of him immediately. "Bully for you. Tell you what, Chester—I've had a long drive, it's raining, and I want to go inside where it's dry. So let's dispense with the good-neighbor routine, okay, and cut to the chase. What do you want?''

As putdowns went, it was a masterpiece, Courtney thought, maybe even suitable for framing—and she was too tired to feel sorry for being deliberately mean to the man.

She expected him to drop his hand, and he did.

She also expected him to lose his smile, but he fooled her there.

His grin only widened, and she could tell he was

going to ignore her sarcasm even before he spoke. "That's Adam, not Chester. Adam Richardson. Although I can understand your mistake. The two names are so similar. Had a long drive, you said? What's your name?"

So much for my supposed mastery of ego-piercing sarcasm, Courtney thought, feeling herself beginning to do a slow burn. She'd have to give him the full treatment, pull out all the stops. Drawing herself up to her most rigidly imperious posture, and as she stood rather tall in the four-inch heels she was wearing she knew she could carry off the look, she pronounced coldly, "*I'm* Courtney Blackmun."

"And *you're* not," Adam responded immediately, the soft rumbling chuckle that accompanied the words setting Courtney's teeth on edge.

"Meaning?" she asked blankly, feeling the cold rain begin to run down the back of her neck. It was impossible. This Adam Richardson character actually hadn't recognized her name! She hadn't been able to write for six months—not six *years*. Lord, Courtney thought, grimacing, how soon they forgot! "Could you please explain that?"

He smiled at her again, and this time his smile intrigued her more than it angered her—which only angered her more. "It's just the way you said your name. You know—'*I'm* Courtney Blackmun...and *you're* not.' Oh, never mind. It was just a joke. You understand jokes, don't you?"

"I understand *humor,* Mr. Richardson," Courtney countered curtly, stepping past him to insert the key in the lock—and to hide her own smile. She was beginning to like Adam Richardson, which meant she'd better get away from him as fast as she could. She was here to work, not to make new friends. "Now, if you'll excuse me?" She pushed open the door and stepped inside.

"Want some help with your luggage?"

Couldn't he take a hint? Courtney took a deep breath in through her nose and held it, sure that when she exhaled, the air would come out in the form of steam. Steam would be all that she would have left. His winsome smile had already drenched her dragonly fire.

"Thank you, no," she answered without turning around, hoping a polite refusal would work better than sarcasm or insults—both of which had been remarkable only for their lack of impact on the man. "It's terribly kind of you to offer, but I think I'll wait until the rain stops. Goodbye. It was nice meeting you, Mr. Richardson."

"Adam."

She turned back to look at him one last time. Yes, her brain registered without her consent, he had wonderful eyes. "It was nice meeting you, *Adam*," she repeated.

Her first steps into the foyer of the condo were like walking into a deep freeze. Suzi had told her she'd make sure the heat would be turned on before Courtney's arrival. She should have known better than to trust her friend, a woman who might be a bitingly incisive, intelligent reviewer, but also a woman who regularly forgot her own phone number. "Oh, Lord, it's even damper in here than it is outside!"

Courtney didn't realize it, but she had issued an invitation—or at least it seemed Adam Richardson thought so. "The heat's probably turned down to maintenance level, just high enough to keep the water pipes from freezing," he explained, stepping past her to head down the hallway, his yellow slicker dripping water everywhere.

"Hey! Where do you think you're going?" Courtney exclaimed, looking on in disbelief. "I wasn't issuing a call for help. I'm capable of finding the thermostat by myself."

"The setup is probably the same for both units," he called over his shoulder as Courtney watched him open a utility closet and reach inside. A moment later she heard the soft clicks of a hot-water heater and the thermostat switching on. "There. That ought to do it. Don't run your bath for at least a half hour," he suggested, turning back to face her.

As he walked toward her he slipped the heavy hood from his head, and Courtney grabbed the doorknob to steady herself. She made a mental note to apologize to Suzi for what she thought the woman had done. No cousin could ever look this good! The gray eyes that had first caught her notice, combined with the even white teeth that he showed almost constantly, were only the beginning of Adam Richardson's physical attributes.

His hair was black, as black as her own, and very thick, brushed haphazardly across his head from a side part, with a few locks tumbling carelessly onto his wide clear brow. His eyebrows were just as dark as his hair, and almost winglike as they soared above his elongated gray eyes. She hadn't noticed the slashes in his cheeks that appeared whenever he smiled, or the deep laugh lines around his eyes that showed her that this was a man who smiled often, but they made an impact on her now, causing her to swallow hard on a sudden lump in her throat.

There was no getting around it. Adam Richardson was one gorgeous hunk of man. But there was more to him than that. Courtney had spent her life looking below the surface, always searching for bits and pieces of human behavior to form into characters in her books, and she could sense immediately that Adam was more than just another pretty face.

He was very self-assured, rather than cocky, for one thing. That meant he had either money or power—or both.

As he shook himself out of the slicker—without an invitation to do so, she noted silently—he exposed a light blue oxford shirt and dark gray cotton slacks that had that wonderfully rumpled look impossible to achieve from clothes bought from a place that offers blue light specials.

His clothes, even his well-worn loafers—worn without socks, of course—had been fashioned by top-of-the-line designers, and his slim-hipped wide-shouldered body wore them with ease.

Oh, yes. Self-confidence, looks, power and money.

Adam Richardson had all those things—and much, much more.

He was now standing in front of her, the slicker folded over one arm, looking at her expectantly. "Well?" she questioned, annoyed that, tall as she was, she still had to raise her head to look into his eyes. "What do you want now? Applause? I would have found the switches eventually."

He tipped his head slightly to one side, as if considering her question. "A simple thank-you would be sufficient, if you think you can get your tongue around something that isn't insulting."

He could dish it out as well as take it, she concluded, her estimation of the man going up yet another notch. Courtney felt herself blush. "Thank you, Adam," she said quietly, her head bowed. She should be ashamed of herself. She was taking out her bad humor on him, and it wasn't his fault.

"There, that wasn't so hard, was it?" Adam asked, and she could hear the laughter in his voice.

She instantly bridled. She might not be a dragon but she wasn't a mouse, either. "Is there anything else, Adam, or may I feel free to see the rest of the condo now?"

He shrugged. "I don't know. You could say 'thank you' again, I suppose. It sounded very nice the first time. And maybe a hot cup of coffee after I've taken care of the luggage you're now going to let me bring in for you so I can hear you say 'thank you, Adam' again," he suggested. "I've been out walking on the beach, and I'm chilled to the bone."

"You can't blame me for that," Courtney countered quickly, knowing she was switching from hot to cold faster than a New York Indian summer, but was somehow unable to help herself. She refused to believe she was even slightly insulted because he hadn't known who she was when she had introduced herself. "You look old enough to know when it's time to come in out of the rain. Everybody else in this burg sure does."

"Is that a New York accent I detect in those dulcet tones? Between Lexington Avenue and the Park, I imagine. It would explain a lot," Adam said, slipping back into his slicker.

"And what do you mean by that?" Courtney eyed him through narrowed lids. He might smile a lot, this Adam Richardson, but he also seemed to know how to bite. "Do you think I'm a snob?"

"I think you're tired," he answered smoothly, "and could use a cup of coffee. You'll probably want to use the bedroom on your left, so I'll put your luggage in there while you see if there's any coffee in the kitchen. There are three bedrooms down here, but that one's got its' own bathroom. The general living quarters are upstairs, off the deck, so that you have a better view of the ocean. Keys still in the ignition?"

"Keys?" she returned blankly, still fascinated by his gray eyes. They had small silver flecks in them, she was sure of it.

"Car keys, Courtney. I need them to get into the trunk."

Just when was it that she had lost control of the situation? The exact moment power had shifted from her to him was unclear. The only thing Courtney knew for sure was that Adam was now calling the shots.

As she heard the snap and click of the heating units coming to life, she nodded, making a decision. "My computer and printer are in the black-watch plaid canvas bags. Leave them there until later, please, as they're allergic to water. Black or white?"

Now she had him confused. She watched, fascinated, as the winglike brows dive-bombed inward toward the bridge of his thin, straight, aristocratic nose. "Black or white what?"

"Your coffee," she said, smiling for the first time. "That's how they say it in jolly old England. Do you want your coffee black, or with cream? Sugar, to a dedicated coffee drinker, isn't even an option."

He zipped up the slicker. "Black. There's probably some instant coffee somewhere in the kitchen upstairs if the condo's been used lately, but unless you've got groceries out in the trunk I doubt that there's anything but powdered cream, anyway. You'll have to go shopping later. There's a supermarket down around Thirty-fourth Street. Be back in a flash."

Courtney watched as he pulled up his hood and dashed back out into the downpour, sliding his long frame in behind the wheel in order to retrieve the keys to the trunk. She felt an almost overwhelming urge to slam the door behind him and lock it.

She had been too quick to write off Adam Richardson as unimportant. The man was dangerous, she was sure of it—even after such short acquaintance. Not dangerous in the usual sense of the word; he wasn't going to rob her, or attack her. She doubted that he'd even be a pest, constantly knocking on her door to borrow a cup of sugar or some such ridiculousness.

No, he was dangerous to Courtney's peace of mind, to her hard-fought-for sense of self-control and self-containment—her self-sufficiency. He was the sort of man a woman wanted to lean on, the sort of man who encouraged a woman to lean on him.

Right now she was too fragile, too delicate to allow herself to be in the company of a strong man like Adam, and she knew it. She would be polite, give him some coffee, and then shut him outside of the condo and outside of her head.

"Because Courtney Blackmun leans on *nobody*," she told herself, mounting the spiral staircase to the kitchen.

Chapter Two

I'm Courtney Blackmun had green eyes, Adam remembered as he raised the trunk lid, watching the collected rainwater cascade onto the cement driveway and his already soaked loafers. He had always been partial to green eyes.

Green eyes reminded him of his cat, Festus, the gray-and-white tiger he'd had as a child in Basking Ridge. Adam had read somewhere that a cat would only look away from you, or close its eyes, if it trusted you completely. He had liked to get down on the carpet in front of Festus and engage the feline in a staring match, only to watch, fascinated, as Festus slowly let his lids squeeze together, and fell asleep.

Trust was important. A man had to be able to look unflinchingly into another person's eyes, knowing that the person was looking back at him, searching for a reason, even an excuse, to trust.

You couldn't fake it, you couldn't don some sort of special many-colored cloak of trust, go out into the world and expect people to buy what you were selling. It didn't work that way—or if it did, it didn't last. It had to be real, if it was to count for anything, if *he* was to count for anything.

If the day ever came that he felt he was putting on an act, deliberately staring people down as he had done with Festus, as if the whole thing was nothing more than a game, then Adam Richardson would turn his back and walk away from it all.

At least he had always thought he would. He still liked to believe he would. Long ago he had promised himself that he would use his power—his ability to influence people, to bring them around to his way of thinking—only for the best, most lofty reasons.

But he also knew, now more than ever, that power was a tricky, sometimes self-deceiving thing. "Power tends to corrupt," Lord Acton had written so many years ago, "and absolute power corrupts absolutely."

Adam had vowed long ago never to forget that warning. But it had been hard, during the long months of the campaign, to withstand the flattery, the hype, the adulation that had seemed to follow him everywhere. My God, there had even been members of Adam Richardson fan clubs at some of his appearances—women of all ages screaming for him as if he was the latest rock star. It was heady stuff!

Now, with so much of it behind him and the real world before him, he couldn't help wondering if it had been his name, his face, his damnably trustworthy smile, or his real accomplishments that had gotten him to the top of the hill.

What he needed, what he wanted, more than a respite from the hubbub on a deserted New Jersey beach, was to find out if Adam Richardson still existed.

Adam smiled. He certainly didn't seem to exist for Courtney Blackmun. Oh, she knew he was alive. He had seen to that, admiring her spunk, as well as her fiery temper, when he had refused to do as she wanted and leave her alone. But she didn't know who he was—a situation he was beginning to believe might be just what he needed to help him get his feet back on the ground.

And, he remembered wryly, he didn't know who she was, either. Although he usually believed in the adage What's fair is fair, he knew that his ignorance of her identity was a lapse he would have to rectify as soon as possible.

He also knew he was attracted to *I'm Courtney Blackmun,* which seemed to be as good a reason as any to use his power to learn her identity, thereby at least temporarily gaining the upper hand.

"Lord Acton sure knew what he was talking about," Adam said, sighing. "I ought to be ashamed of myself—but I'm not."

Hefting the three heavy suitcases out of the trunk, pushing the smallest one beneath his left arm, Adam deliberately laughed out loud at the thought that he had known Courtney Blackmun less than one hour and already the woman had him talking to himself.

And why had he been going all profound on himself, anyway? He was here to clear his mind, blow away the cobwebs and get ready for January. This wasn't a time for deep thinking—or even for the pursuit of a beautiful woman. It was a time he had deliberately set aside for relaxation, a time to give his mind a break. What had brought all this on, anyway?

"Green eyes," he reminded himself aloud, setting down a suitcase in order to slam the trunk lid shut. "You really do need a rest, Richardson, if Courtney Blackmun's beautiful come-hither green eyes remind you of trust and duty. Now you *know* you've been working too hard!"

He walked past the still-open front door of the condo, kicking it shut behind him as he headed for the main bedroom. He had done as she had ordered, leaving the two black-watch plaid cases in the trunk. But now, as he heard her moving about above him in the kitchen of the two-story condo, opening and closing cabinet doors on what sounded like a search-and-destroy mission, he gave himself a moment to think about them.

She had told him the cases contained her computer and printer. Why would Courtney need a computer? She sure as hell didn't look like an accountant, or any business executive he had ever encountered. Not that he was a chauvinist, he assured himself. He knew beauty and brains weren't mutually exclusive. Beatrice was proof of that.

But it was more than Courtney Blackmun's beauty and intelligence that intrigued him. She had a definite air about her, a nervous, brittle sort of protective

shell—a nearly detectable Hands Off sign hanging
around her gorgeous slim throat. She was no cat, de-
spite her mysterious emerald eyes. She was more like
a high-strung thoroughbred, sleek and beautiful and
very, very expensive, but also vulnerable, alert to danger and capable of being more than a little dangerous.

And, God, was she beautiful! She was tall, for one
thing, and being tall himself, Adam liked the idea that
the top of her head came to his shoulder, not that he
could have overpowered her if she just tipped five feet
in her stockinged feet. He was already convinced
Courtney Blackmun knew how to take care of herself.

Then there was her hair, a glorious tumble of soft
touchable ebony that caressed the perfect oval of her
face and cascaded onto her straight shoulders. Her fa-
cial features were patrician, but the slight humanizing
tilt to her nose and the betraying fullness of her bottom
lip assured him that her air of jaded sophistication was
nothing more than another form of self-protection.

Which led him back to his confusion over the computer in her trunk. Courtney Blackmun. Courtney
Blackmun. He turned the name over and over in his
mind with the niggling feeling that he had heard it
somewhere. She had been surprised when he hadn't
recognized her name—maybe even as surprised as he
had been when she hadn't recognized his—although
she had covered that surprise with a quick insult.

Yes, he had to know. He'd phone Beatrice, his res-
ident fountain of information, when he got back to his
own condo. Beatrice, bless her, knew everything.

"Hey, Chester! If you're done poking through my suitcases, the coffee's ready."

Adam looked up at the ceiling, Courtney's invitation-cum-accusation slamming him back to reality. It was time to get back in the battle. He headed into the hallway and climbed the carpeted spiral metal staircase to the upper floor, walking through the living room to the small dining room.

"Sorry about that," he said, his smile deliberately sheepish as he slid into a chair across the table from where Courtney sat and wrapped both hands around a thick white mug of steaming coffee. "Sometimes my mind tends to drift off on its own without my realizing it."

"I know the feeling."

Ah, she had smiled as she answered him. A smile was always good. Maybe the battle was over. Maybe things were looking up. Adam took his first sip of the hot liquid, relaxing as the warmth hit his chilled insides. "That's what's so great about a place like this in the off-season. You can walk around, your head in the clouds, without fear of the men in the white coats coming to take you away somewhere to weave baskets."

Courtney laughed out loud. "You, too? There are times when my mind goes off on a tangent, and I come back to my senses only to find the people I'm with looking at me in the strangest way."

Adam hid his eyes from her as he took another sip of coffee. Yes, things were *definitely* looking up. "So," he said, putting down his cup and trying to keep his voice casual as he purposely uttered the old cliché, "You come here often?"

She shook her head. "First time, actually. The condo belongs to a friend. You?"

She had answered his question, he'd give her that, but she hadn't really told him anything. And she had just as quickly turned the tables on him, asking him a question. *She's smooth*, he warned himself, leaning back on the chair so that the front legs lifted off the carpet.

Well, two could play at that game. "Looks like we're both first timers. The condo belongs to a friend of mine," he answered, then decided to give her more. "My friend Beatrice. She said it was a great place to hide out for a while."

My, Grandma, what big eyes you have, Adam thought, smothering a smile as Courtney's eyes widened for a fraction of a second before she lowered her absurdly long, sooty lashes and took a sip of the rapidly cooling coffee. The heat was on, but the condo was still decidedly chilly and she had not yet taken off her coat.

When she spoke her voice was coolly unaffected. "So, you're on the lam, are you, Adam? I thought I detected a certain shiftiness around your eyes."

"No such luck, Courtney," Adam answered amicably. "Being on the lam sounds like it could be fun, even if I do resent that crack about my eyes. I'm just here on, er, a vacation, till the first of the year—if Beatrice can keep her mouth shut and nobody finds out where I am."

"A top executive taking a break from the corporate grind, or are you hiding out from an angry board of directors?"

He leaned back until the top of the chair pressed against the wall. Adam felt his spine stiffening as a sudden attack of stubbornness overcame him. If she didn't know—and it looked more and more as if she really didn't know—then he was damned if he was going to tell her! "No business for me, Courtney," he said flippantly. "I'm strictly a man of leisure."

"You don't work?" Adam noticed a definite chill invading Courtney's voice, her few moments of guarded friendliness abruptly disappearing behind a disapproving frown.

He didn't work? No, only twenty-six hours a day, eight days a week. Deciding to let her believe what she wanted, he returned easily, "Work? Perish the thought. I don't have to, thank God. I made my money the old-fashioned way, Courtney. I inherited it." He narrowed his eyes to gauge her response to his somewhat irreverent answer.

Ah, and now the iceman cometh, he told himself, watching as Courtney fairly leapt to her feet, snatching both coffee cups from the table and disappearing into the kitchen.

"Thank you so much for helping with my luggage, Adam," she called out to him as, with a vengeance, she turned on the water in the double sink, "but I really am exhausted from the drive. I'm sure you know your way out."

Adam let the front legs of his chair back down on

the carpet. He probably should tell her the truth before he landed himself with a terminal case of Courtney frostbite, but a part of him was intrigued by her sudden change of attitude. It was just as intriguing as the rest of her.

Courtney Blackmun wasn't going to fawn all over him because he was, as one newspaper editorial said, "a rising star." And wasn't that what he wanted— someone to be totally honest with him? Someone to like or dislike him just because of who he was, and not judge him or feign friendliness because of what he was? Someone who wasn't going to gush, or fawn, or feign interest because she wanted something from him?

"I guess dinner is out of the question," he said with deliberate cheekiness, standing and looking at her across the serving bar that divided the kitchen and dining room. "Was it something I said?"

"Go straight to the head of the class, Adam," Courtney told him, the cloud of steam rising from the stainless-steel sink, showing him that the hot-water heater had kicked in right on schedule. "We have nothing in common. *I'm* not in Ocean City to hide from Bunky and Binky."

Wow! Adam felt as if he had unwittingly lit the fuse to a dozen-stick bundle of dynamite. He almost laughed out loud. "Did you really say Bunky and Binky?"

She tipped the water out of the cups and transferred them, bottoms up, to the other side of the sink. "All right then, Muffy and Buffy. Surely at least one of those names fits the gang your sort hangs out with as you globe hop on Daddy's money?''

"Let me get this straight," Adam said, walking around the bar to enter the kitchen. "You don't like me because I'm wealthy?"

"You're only half-right," she told him, turning so that she was leaning against the sink, her hands on the edge of the counter.

"Okay. Let me run this one past you. You don't like me because I'm wealthy—and I don't work?"

"Bingo. You may start out slow, Chester, but you catch on fast. Your kind makes me sick."

Adam leaned against the counter and scratched his head. "Now, that's a switch. Excuse me if I appear dense, but it's usually the other way around. You know, money as an aphrodisiac. And there are a lot of women who think a life of leisure—even on inherited money—is not to be whistled down the wind."

Courtney dried her hands and threw the towel in the sink. "Not to me. Trite as it may seem, I still believe that *I'm* the one who is making my money the old-fashioned way. You see, Chester, old bunkie—I *earn* it."

And with that, Courtney turned on her heel and headed for the staircase. Precisely five seconds later he heard the door to her bedroom slam shut.

"My, oh my, Chester, old man," Adam told himself as he headed for the staircase and the front door, "I think this is going to prove to be *very* interesting!"

Courtney stood at the wide wall of windows, looking out over the long wooden deck that stretched to-

ward the deserted beach and the slate-gray waters of
a stormy Atlantic. It was just past dawn and a host of
loud screeching gulls were swooping across the beach,
on the lookout for breakfast. Three of the sea gulls, at
least, had already discovered a gourmet meal in the
form of a beached horseshoe crab, although it seemed
that they were spending more time guarding their prize
from the other birds than dining on it.

Taking a sip of coffee from the mug in her hand,
Courtney continued to watch the sea gulls, something
in their aggressive attitude reminding her of the talk-
show host she had locked horns with in Duluth six
months earlier. "Except the sea gulls have more pleasant voices," she decided, turning away from the window.

The living room of the condo was arranged with a
conversation area furnished with an overstuffed couch
and love seat, with several small assorted chairs scat-
tered around the room in a curiously abandoned way.
It was obvious that Suzi had begun decorating with
the conversation area firmly in her mind, then left the
rest of the furniture to figure out its own purpose.

There was a small brick corner fireplace in the L-
shaped area to the left of the spiral staircase, and
Courtney wished she could find some wood to burn in
it. Fires were supposed to be cheery. Cheery sounded
like something she'd like to be—especially after the
restless night she had spent thinking about Adam
Richardson.

She had been rude to the man—needlessly rude—

but he had rubbed her the wrong way. She was feeling too vulnerable right now, too fragile, to have to deal with a man who, because of circumstance, never had to worry about money or work. Adam Richardson was a man who wouldn't know what it was like to feel as if his professional legs had been cut out from under him when he wasn't looking.

Work. Her stomach was instantly queasy as fear of facing the blank screen on her computer made her break out in a cold sweat. Yes, it was time to try to get to work—or she would end up weaving baskets in some cozy rest home.

Carrying her coffee mug with her, she descended the spiral staircase to the ground floor, passed by the bedroom in which she had tossed and turned the previous night and entered the larger of the two remaining bedrooms.

Her computer was sitting on the desk in front of the blank wall to which she had dragged it at midnight last night, knowing that its previous placement, in front of a window looking out over the ocean, would only give her yet another excuse to daydream. She was here to work, damn it, not watch the ocean as it sent wave after hypnotic wave tumbling against the shore.

The computer stared back at her, its single, square now-black eye silently mocking her. She knew the computer was an inanimate object, but she had not yet overcome the idea that not only did it record her thoughts, it assessed them, as well.

Just last month, after struggling for hours over a particularly difficult passage, the computer screen had turned dark, only to have a small, computer-shaped icon appear on the screen, with X's for eyes, and, she swore, its tongue sticking out at her. No matter how hard she tried, she couldn't get the computer to cough up the passage. It was gone forever.

"It's like having a built-in editor," she said, sitting down in front of the dark screen and gingerly flipping the switch to On. "The passage stank to high heaven, only I didn't want to admit it. And everything I've tried to write for the past six months has been just as bad. Maybe I should go back to writing longhand in notebooks."

The screen lit to a light gray and Courtney watched while the computer-shaped icon appeared, its blinking question mark silently asking what she wanted. Slipping in the start-up disk, she waited again while the computer spun it around, taking the information it needed to ready the word-processing program for operation.

"Well, that's the easy part done," Courtney said, sighing as she reached for a second disk and inserted it in the external disk drive. The icon for that disk, already labeled *Questions of the Heart*, positioned itself to the right of the screen.

"Great title," she told herself. "A really first-rate title. An eye-catching thought-provoking title. Now if only I knew what the hell it meant." She pressed the hand control twice, opening the disk, and thirty seconds later she was looking at the first page of her new novel.

"Big deal," she groused. "I'm also looking at the *last* page."

Sitting back, she reached into her pocket and took out her cigarette case, lighting the first of what stretched into half a pack over the next two hours, as she tried to concentrate on developing a newer, fresher, more workable plot.

Courtney sat forward abruptly as a coherent thought penetrated her brain, which she had begun to believe had been switched to Stun the moment she had turned on the computer. *Elliot had gray eyes.* Hey, how about that! Only one day in Ocean City, and already she'd had a breakthrough. Her fingers flying, Courtney typed this information into the computer. She hadn't known he had gray eyes. Six months—and she hadn't known her hero had gray eyes.

No, wait a minute. Elliot didn't have gray eyes. The *villain* had gray eyes. Oh, yes, she could see the villain very clearly now. He had black hair, and gray eyes, and very white teeth. The villain—who was after the heroine's money—was finally coming to life. No, scratch that. He didn't want her money; he lusted after her virtue. Whatever he was after, she could see him clearly in her mind's eye.

Okay, so where had Elliot gone—her hero with the blank Little Orphan Annie eyes? And just how did he figure into the picture?

He didn't, damn it.

She lit another cigarette. And another. And another. Courtney finally shut down the computer at noon, having stared at that same first page and the blinking cursor for nearly five discouraging hours.

It wasn't that she hadn't written anything, for she had been able to type out a few preliminary notes. She just hadn't bothered to save them on disk, grateful for the computer's ability to erase forever the strained obviously forced thoughts that had come from no place and traveled nowhere.

"Maybe I should drive up the coast and see if I can get a job hustling drinks on the floor of one of the casinos," she mused, closing the door on the computer's mocking dark eye. "Anything is better than this."

She climbed the stairs to drift aimlessly through the kitchen, which she had stocked with six bags of groceries obtained last night from the nearby supermarket. Nothing appealed to her, and she shut the refrigerator door on two pounds of assorted lunch meats. If nothing else, she was shedding those five pounds the spring book tour had added to her frame.

She looked toward the door that led out onto the deck. The last of the clouds had blown away and the sun was shining on the water. The ocean had turned a deep midnight blue, with small white-edged waves caressing rather than pounding against the shore. Before she could stop herself, she picked up her coat from the back of the love seat and stepped out onto the deck, quietly rejoicing in the fact that a high wall separated her deck from Adam's.

The first thing she noticed was the fresh briny smell of the water. As a stiff breeze coming inland off the ocean lifted her hair away from her shoulders and the noonday sun warmed her cheeks, she took several deep cleansing breaths, trying to remove any lingering residue of tobacco smoke from her lungs.

Walking to the far edge of the wide deck, she spread her hands on the railing and looked out over the ocean, amazed that, having spent the morning as tense as an overwound watch, she could actually feel her taut muscles relaxing. A smile tickled at the corners of her mouth as she gloried in the moment.

After a few minutes of blessed peace, Courtney decided to go down to the beach, suddenly obsessed with the notion of writing her name in the hard wet sand near the shoreline. It was a silly idea, she registered rationally—maybe even juvenile—but it was something she wanted to do. Then, after making herself some sort of lunch, she would unearth a beach chair from the ground-floor storage room and sit on the deck, watching her handiwork melt away beneath the incoming tide.

She tripped down the shallow wooden steps, almost losing her balance as her sneakered feet made their first contact with the soft dry sand at the bottom of the steps. Laughing out loud at the sudden jolt to her system, she started walking toward the breaking waves, her feet moving faster and faster as the harder flatter sand on the beach made her feel as if she was on a racetrack.

Turning this way and that as she ran, gulls screaming above her head, she spied a narrow twisted length of driftwood lying half-buried in the sand. It would make a perfect pen for beach-writing. Picking it up, she approached the shoreline slowly, her interest caught again by the wide variety of shells and small, smooth-colored stones that littered the beach.

Crouching down on her haunches, her hair blowing across her eyes, she began picking up some of the wet sand-dusted stones, planning to fill a jar with them so that she'd always be reminded of this very private interlude on a deserted Ocean City beach.

Once her pockets were full, Courtney picked up her ''pen'' again and scratched her name across the beach in letters more than two feet high, then stood back to admire her handiwork. It wasn't a professional printing job, and the *m* in Blackmun was a disaster, but she was pleased just the same. She had made her mark here, on this beach, and now it would be hers—at least until the tide came in.

Making her mark. That had been important to Courtney for as long as she could remember. It wasn't enough to merely exist; her existence had to *mean* something, had to count for something. Maybe it was because she had been an orphan, with no past, no family, that she had always felt this need to imprint her own special mark on life.

For a while Courtney had believed she could live her life through other people; through her young husband, Rob, and then their daughter, Sydney—her own little family.

But Rob had died, leaving her with a nine-month-old infant and no money, no real education and no way to make a living. It had suddenly, brutally, become hard for the then nineteen-year-old Courtney to exist at all.

She knew, and had vowed never to forget, how far she had come, and how hard it had been to get there. And she was never, ever, going back. The need to matter, to exist, to have some say in her own life and the life of her daughter—that was the carrot that had driven her to write fourteen books in ten years.

Never again would she let circumstances control her. She would control her own circumstances.

If she never wrote another word, she would have enough money for her and Sydney to live in reasonable comfort for the rest of their lives, not that Harry would be too thrilled if she retired. As thoughts of her increasingly demanding agent threatened to destroy her small newfound oasis of peace, Courtney deliberately pushed them out of her mind.

Yes, she had to exist for a reason, but that reason wasn't to earn money. Money had ceased to be an incentive before she'd had enough of it to feel secure. She was a writer, a damn good writer, who wrote damn good books! Her books may have begun as a means to an end, a way out of poverty for Sydney and herself after Rob's death, but they were also as important to her as the air she breathed.

"It's not even as if I have a choice," she explained to a nearby sea gull as she began walking up the beach without really knowing where she was going, her hands jammed into her coat pockets, her fingers wrapped around the hard cold of the still-wet stones. "I *have* to write, just as much as I have to breathe."

She wiped at her cheeks, blaming the wind for the sudden stinging she felt behind her eyes. "I can't have lost it. Dear God, I can't have lost it! I *have* to write!"

She walked until she lost sight of the beach house that contained Suzi's condo, until the invigorating chill of the sunny November day became a teeth-rattling cold, until she had won some small measure of peace with herself, before turning back the way she had come.

As she approached the area behind the condo she could see that the tide had not yet begun toward her lettering, and with a sudden rumbling of her protesting stomach, she remembered that she had planned to eat lunch on the deck while watching the tide roll in. She stopped, facing the ocean for one last look before heading back to the steps.

"Beautiful, isn't it? I walk the beach two or three times a day, no matter what the weather."

Courtney's hands closed convulsively around the small piles of stones in her pockets as she struggled to retain her composure. Adam's voice had come to her out of nowhere, shattering her hard-won peace into a million jagged-edged splinters. Turning slowly, she wasn't surprised to see him standing just two feet behind her, his hands deep in the pockets of a teal-blue windbreaker with a yacht club insignia embroidered, not stamped, on the left chest pocket.

The front of his hair was blowing about in the well-ordered casualness only an excellent cut could provide, and the soft-collared cotton golf shirt that rose above the windbreaker was startlingly white against his deep tan. She refused to look lower, knowing his slacks and shoes would likewise be perfect. He was so perfect, as a matter of fact, that she longed to punch him in the mouth.

And he had gray eyes—just like the villain in *Questions of the Heart*! No wonder she had felt that small spurt of inspiration this morning. Adam Richardson would make a perfect villain—and he would definitely have to be after her heroine's virtue!

"Would a handful of small stones, if there were enough of them, that is, double for brass knuckles or a fistful of quarters, do you think?" Courtney inquired sweetly, enjoying the way Adam's smile faltered.

But he recovered quickly, she had to hand him that. Within a moment the smile was back, a smile that reached all the way to his maddeningly attractive, all-seeing gray eyes. "I never sleep well my first night in a new bed, either," Adam said commiseratingly, as if apologizing for her rudeness. "You hungry, Courtney? I've got a full pot of sloppy joe simmering on the stove. Homemade, by the way, as I consider myself to be a pretty decent cook."

"You're not real good at taking a hint, though, are you?" Courtney countered, shaking her head as she watched the laugh lines deepen beside his curious eyes. "Oh, what the hell," she said, taking the arm he had offered her, "I guess it'll be easier to amuse you, then maybe I can get back to work."

"Another bestseller in the works?" Adam asked as he led her toward the flight of wooden steps that climbed to the deck on his side of the beach house.

She didn't miss a beat, her footsteps never faltering as she measured them to match Adam's long ones stride for stride. She wouldn't give him the satisfaction of knowing he had surprised her. "First cooking—and now you're a private eye. My goodness, is there no end to your talents, Adam? You certainly have been a busy little bee. Who told you, or did you figure it out on your own?"

"You say that as if you'd find it hard to believe I could have figured it out by myself," he commented, opening the door to the condo. "As a matter of fact, I wouldn't be surprised if you believe I can't walk and chew gum at the same time. I assure you, Courtney, I've been allowed out on my own for quite some time now."

"Sorry, Adam," Courtney apologized, knowing she was sincerely sorry only as she heard herself say the words. What was it about the man that immediately brought out the worst in her? The word *fear* crept unwanted into her head, as it had the first time she had met him, but quickly she shooed it away. That was ridiculous. She wasn't afraid of Adam. Maybe it was just her reaction to him that she feared.

"That's all right, Courtney," he answered easily, interrupting her train of thought. For that she was instantly grateful, as she hadn't liked the direction those thoughts were taking her. "I asked for it, sneaking up behind you while you were communing with nature."

She looked around the living room as she entered, seeing that even though the physical setup was the same on Suzi's side of the building the condos were distinctively different. His side was furnished with old-world French charm, lovely wood furniture, and a plethora of knickknacks—some of them real antiques, some of them screaming of boardwalk souvenir shops.

"Definitely borrowed from a friend," she said, picking up a particularly homely tray with the words, *Ocean City, America's first choice in family resorts* stamped on it. "This place is lovely, but it isn't anything like you."

Adam headed toward the kitchen. "No?" he called over his shoulder as he rid himself of the windbreaker. "You were expecting maybe black velvet couches and lots of mirrors?"

The hunger-pang-inducing aroma of sloppy joe reached out to meet her when she was halfway to the kitchen, and she decided she was being a witch—again. Moving into the kitchen to stand with one hip propped against the counter, she said, "Let's say we call a truce, Chester, okay? After all, it's not your fault that you get on my nerves."

He turned away from the stove, the pot lid in his hand, to wink at her. "You're only saying that because you're coveting my dinner, but I'm not proud. I'll take anything I can get."

Once they were seated at the delicate French Provincial dining-room table, their meals sitting in front of them on red-and-white-checked paper plates, Courtney asked quietly, "Why, Adam?"

"Why?" he repeated solemnly, looking at the sandwich he held in front of him as if it had the answers to all the secrets in the universe. "Why what, Court-

ney? Why is the grass always greener on a golf
course? Why is the sky always clearest after a storm?
Why can't the Yankees win the pennant? Why did I
bother to call good old Beatrice and ask her who you
are? Why in hell do I let you keep calling me Chester?''

"I'm truly sorry about that, Adam. Chester Dingman was the village idiot in my second novel, and I
resurrect him whenever I want to put somebody down.
I guess you could call it my defense system," Courtney explained, trying hard not to giggle. He looked so
silly, squinting at the dripping sandwich. "What I really want to know is why it's important for you to be
with me, considering the fact that I've been anything
but nice to you. Surely you can't be that desperate.''

Chapter Three

Adam looked across the table at Courtney searchingly, trying to gauge her mood. There was a hint of panic in her beautiful green eyes, and her posture reminded him of a small cornered animal—with her every muscle tensed for either fight or flight. And the last thing he wanted from Courtney was her absence. What he said next was important. Very important. Critical, actually.

He opted for an attempt at humor, and what the press had called his Boy Scout look—the one that promised that he was loyal, honest, trustworthy and, as per the Scout oath, "morally straight." Pointing to the messy sandwich in his right hand, he said, "But I *am* that desperate, Courtney. You see, I only know how to cook in quantity, and I was hoping you'd share it with me. If you desert me now, I'll be forced to eat this stuff by myself three meals a day for a week. You wouldn't do that to your good buddy Chester Dingman, would you?''

He could see her relaxing, but only slightly, as she was still staring at him, one dark brow raised quizzically. Obviously she was a believer in the Boy Scout motto: Be Prepared. He watched as she took another bite, chewed it slowly, deliberately, then swallowed before answering him. ''In quantity, huh? Where did you learn how to cook? The army, or a white-collar prison?'' Courtney wiggled her eyebrows at him, her comical expression taking any sting out of her question.

She was fishing again, but he wasn't about to take the bait. He rather liked this new role of mystery man; it was quite a difference from the past year, when he had been forced to justify everything about himself. This was one woman who would have to take him on faith alone.

He schooled his features into a deadly serious expression. ''You got me, Courtney. I'm an ex-Wall Street inside trader, let out early for good behavior. Besides, I kept beating the warden at tennis.''

She laughed at his joke, and something inside his chest, some vital part of him that had been tied in a painful knot, eased. ''And I'm Bonnie Parker,'' she admitted on a sigh, ''hiding out from the feds and my trigger-happy partner, Clyde, who found out I double-crossed him.''

''No, you're not,'' Adam countered, willing to play along with her. ''Bonnie's blond and sort of, um, dead.''

"Sort of, um, dead?" Courtney repeated, reaching for the glass of soda Adam had served to her earlier. "There's nothing 'sort of' about being dead, Chester. It's like being a little bit pregnant. There is no such animal. Hey, either you is or you ain't."

"Ain't? And you're an *author*?" Adam leaned forward, grinning. Courtney was now relaxed enough to spar with him. "To think that Beatrice nearly swooned over the phone when I told her Courtney Blackmun is my next-door neighbor. And let me tell you, bunkie, there's not a whole lot in this wide wacky world that can make Beatrice swoon."

Courtney rose, taking her glass, napkin and empty plate into the kitchen. "Boggles the mind, doesn't it?" she called over her shoulder. "But then you have to remember, *I'm* Courtney Blackmun."

Adam brought up the rear, carrying his own plate and glass. "Do you think I could have your autograph for Beatrice—maybe on one of these napkins? I think she'd trample me to get it, although she'd never ask me to do it," he told her, dumping his garbage in the trash can under the sink.

"A napkin, Adam? I think I have a copy of one of my books in my luggage. I'll autograph that for her," Courtney told him, looking around the kitchen as if hunting for the garbage can.

"Great! Here, let me take that. Nobody said you had to work for your lunch." He reached out to take the paper plate from her hand at the same moment she bent to discard it. Their fingers met—just like in the movies, he thought randomly—sending an unexpected jolt through Adam's system from his head to his toes. He looked down at their hands, half expecting to see tiny lightning bolts shooting out from the ends of his fingers, so electric was her touch.

He looked up straight into Courtney's eyes and tried to determine if she had felt the same shock. If she had, she hid her emotions well—definitely better than he did, for he knew he hadn't hidden his reaction with his usual expertise. It was only when she spoke that he could believe she hadn't been totally unaffected by the small incident.

"I—I have to be going now, Adam," she said, the slight stammer and faintly tremulous tone of her voice unknowingly doing wonders for his ego. "I've got to work."

This small encouragement from her prompted him to try getting yet another step closer to her. He slipped an arm around Courtney's waist, saying softly, "I'll walk you back."

Her escape from his slight impersonal embrace was so fluid, so graceful, that he couldn't actually say that she had meant to give him a silent "hands off" message. "That's not necessary, Adam. Really. I don't think I'm in danger of getting lost. But thanks for the lunch. It was delicious. If you ever need a reference, look me up."

There was nothing left to do but give in gracefully. Besides, she was already at the door to the deck, her hand on the knob. He couldn't grab hold of her and forcefully keep her here, could he? But he wanted to, he really did want to.

"How about dinner tonight at one of the local restaurants?" he asked nonchalantly, crossing his fingers behind his back while wondering why her answer meant so much to him. When her green eyes clouded he pressed on, "You're not going to consign me to more sloppy joe and my own boring company, are you? I mean, think of the good-neighbor policy and all that stuff. Think of my cholesterol level."

She sighed, then shook her head. "Not tonight, Adam. Eat a tossed salad with it, and don't put it on a roll. I—I really do have to work. Honestly."

He leaned against the back of a mauve wing chair, crossing his arms against his chest. "You say that as if you're dreading it. Are you behind on a deadline or something?"

"Or something," Courtney told him, opening the door, and he sensed that he had somehow struck yet another nerve. She took one step out onto the deck before turning back to ask, "This Beatrice of yours. What's she like? I mean, other than the fact that she doesn't smoke—at least I didn't see any ashtrays—puts French Provincial furniture in beach houses and collects antiques."

Chalk one up for the good guys! Adam thought triumphantly, pushing himself away from the chair. "Beatrice? My Beatrice?" he asked, deliberately keeping his voice neutral. "Why do you ask?"

She lowered her eyelashes, and he was sure she was going to lie. "Why, to pattern my autograph to her, of course. I—I like to be personal with autographs when I can, and I thought, if I could get a mental picture of her I could, you know, do it better.''

"Do it better," Adam repeated, nodding as if he believed her. "Okay. Let me think. How would I describe Beatrice? I couldn't function without her, that's for sure. And she wouldn't let me—that's also for sure. Lord, how I love that woman!"

"I see," Courtney said woodenly, her features frozen into an expressionless mask.

"I mean it," Adam pushed on, enjoying himself. "I would probably fall apart if she ever left me. You might get to meet her if you stay in Ocean City long enough, for I'm sure she'll be down to check up on me before long. I don't know why, but I don't think she trusts me. You'll recognize her immediately. She's a tall sleek blonde with—''

Courtney had turned away, taking another step onto the deck. "You can quit before you get to her vital statistics, Adam. I think I get the picture," she said, waving her hand as if she had heard enough.

"—the body of a teenager, and if she weren't old enough to be my mother I'd have married her years ago," Adam ended, his grin so wide he wondered if it would split his face.

Courtney whirled around to glare at him, her hands on her hips. "You rat!" she exclaimed hotly. "You did that on purpose!"

"Of course I did," Adam agreed honestly. "I admit it. I wanted to see your reaction. My sloppy joe is pretty potent, you know. I thought we were getting along fairly well and decided to see if you liked me for myself or my secret sauce.''

"You or your secret sauce?" She smiled up at him and he felt the thrill of his first small victory. She was beginning to accept him—without benefit of any staff buildup or white papers or advance publicity. "That's a tough one. Can I get back to you on that, Adam?" she asked, walking toward the steps, but slowly, as if she wouldn't mind if he followed her.

He was right. This time, when Adam slipped his arm around her waist, Courtney didn't employ any escape techniques. "Now," he began, as the light floral scent of the perfume she wore did funny things to his equilibrium, "how about a rain check on that dinner?"

Courtney stopped at the bottom of the stairs that led up to the deck on her side of the building. "Thanks for helping me find my way home across the wilds of thirty yards of beach. I couldn't have done it without you," she told Adam, moving to stand on the third step, so that she could look down at him.

She wanted to invite him upstairs but couldn't think of a reason to do so. Besides, she shouldn't encourage him—or herself. "I think I can find my way from here."

He smiled up at her as he placed his left foot on the bottom step and drew one hand across his brow as if wiping away fatigue after fighting a good fight. "That's all right, ma'am, think nothin' of it. It was a dirty job, but I reckon somebody had to do it."

"Nut," she said, laughing at his silliness. He really

was very nice, this Adam Richardson, and he sure could whip up a mean sloppy joe. "Why don't you come upstairs for dessert? There's a chocolate cake I bought at the supermarket that I've been looking for an excuse to cut. But seriously, Adam, I will have to get to work as soon as we're through. If you only knew— Oh, damn! That's my phone, isn't it?"

Without waiting for his answer, Courtney turned on her heel and sprinted up the steps, already running a mental list of possible callers through her head, dissatisfied with each answer her brain shot back at her. Pulling the key out of her jacket pocket, she left the door hanging open behind her as she ran for the kitchen phone before the caller hung up. The only thing worse than having her supposed peace and quiet disturbed would be not knowing who was trying to disturb it.

"Hello!" she gasped into the receiver, trying to recover her breath as she leaned against the low dividing wall between the kitchen and dining room.

"Mrs. Blackmun?" the voice on the other end of the line inquired primly. "This is Mrs. Breckenridge, headmistress of Miss Potter's School. The telephone rang for quite a considerable length of time. I do hope I have not torn you away from something."

The woman's autocratic tone put the lie to her words. That tone clearly indicated that she was reprimanding Courtney for not having picked up the phone on the first ring, and the woman couldn't care less even if she had interrupted Courtney in the middle of performing the Heimlich maneuver on herself. "I'm afraid I have some very disturbing news for you," Mrs. Breckenridge said, her voice switching in tone so as to sound almost sorrowful.

Courtney's mind, which had been pleasurably occupied with thoughts of making Mrs. Breckenridge into a thoroughly unappealing character in her next book, rapidly shifted gears at the woman's last statement. Her heart skipped a beat, then began hammering away at twice its normal rate. "Sydney? Has something happened to Sydney? Is she all right?"

Mrs. Breckenridge's voice turned glacial. "Sydney is quite well, Mrs. Blackmun. It is the rest of us that concerns me. Your daughter, Mrs. Blackmun, is, not to dress the business up in comforting words, completely incorrigible!"

Relief in knowing that Sydney was physically well was quickly replaced with despair. With her left hand still clutching the receiver close to her ear, Courtney buried her head in her right hand, slowly shaking her head.

"Oh, Sydney, Sydney. What have you done now?" she murmured, barely listening as Mrs. Breckenridge began cataloging a list of Sydney's sins, which ranged from the child's instigating a food fight in the cafeteria, to being found in the second-floor bathroom at two in the morning, smoking a cigarette bought from one of the elderly janitors—with whom she was "entirely too familiar." There was nothing else for it, the headmistress told her; Sydney had to be expelled.

When Mrs. Breckenridge's list of complaints finally ran down—and it took a long time, for Sydney had apparently been a busy, busy girl—Courtney tried to reason with the woman. "I know my daughter can be a bit headstrong, Mrs. Breckenridge," she began, hating the pleading tones she heard in her own voice, "but I have explained the circumstances. Sydney is a very bright, highly strung child. I also know that her intelligence and rather precocious nature present a challenge, but your school came highly recommended. Surely, if I might have a talk with her, we can all work together to find some way to—"

"Precocious!" the headmistress broke in, just as Courtney was about to be thoroughly sickened by her own pleading to let Sydney be given another chance. "Is that what you call hanging poor Miss Hardcastle's underwear from the flagpole, Mrs. Blackmun? I don't call that precocious. I call that incorrigible! No, no. We've tried our best. We've worked very diligently with Sydney, but I'm afraid that she just doesn't have what it takes to become a true Miss Potter girl. If she were a boy, Mrs. Blackmun, I would be prone to suggest a good military school."

Courtney's spine stiffened, her hand dropping away from her face as she stared across the kitchen at the second hand of the clock that hung over the sink. The hand moved in small computerized jerks, second by second, almost as if it were counting down to zero, and the explosive lift-off of her temper. "You're labeling my child incorrigible, Mrs. Breckenridge? Do you have any idea how difficult it will be for Sydney to find another school if you do that?" she asked tightly.

"I am quite aware of it," Mrs. Breckenridge began in what must have been her sternest headmistress voice, "but while we are all thrilled with her academic accomplishments, my entire staff has threatened to revolt unless Sydney is removed from their midst."

"Are you trying to tell me that one barely teenage girl is capable of causing a mutiny, Mrs. Breckenridge?" Courtney broke in, suddenly very weary. Besides, what was she arguing about, anyway? She was Sydney's mother—and she knew the child was more than capable of such a thing. "Oh, never mind, Mrs. Breckenridge. I understand. Have you told Sydney of your decision? And when can I pick her up? As you know, I'm not in New York at the moment."

"That's quite all right," the headmistress hurried to assure her. "I've already checked the schedules, and I can have one of our junior teachers accompany Sydney on a bus that arrives in Ocean City via Atlantic City at nine this evening. You can pick her up at the bus station."

"The Ocean City bus station? How terribly, terribly efficient of you, Mrs. Breckenridge," Courtney gritted. "Sydney must really have been in rare form to warrant the bum's rush you're giving her. Very well, I'll accept that arrangement."

There was a short pregnant pause at the other end of the phone before the headmistress spoke again. "We had so hoped, Mrs. Blackmun, considering the great strides we made with Sydney over these past few months, that it wouldn't come to this. She won first honors in our Science Fair, you know, as well as first prize in the annual Miss Potter Poetry Fair." Courtney could hear an audible sigh come down to her through the wires. "I will keep the word *incorrigible* out of Sydney's records. Contrary to what you must be thinking, Mrs. Blackmun, we all like Sydney very much. We just can't live with her."

Courtney took the receiver from her ear for a moment, staring at it in openmouthed astonishment, before pulling it close once more. It still amazed her how Sydney could behave like the worst of brats and still come out of a situation smelling like a rose. Well, maybe not completely smelling like a rose—she had been expelled again, hadn't she? "Thank you, Mrs. Breckenridge. I appreciate that, and I'm sorry Sydney was such a bother. And please—give Miss Hardcastle my condolences on the loss of her underwear. Goodbye."

She waited until the return of the dial tone told her that the headmistress had hung up before her own receiver connected with the wall receptacle so forcefully that the telephone rang once, in vocal protest of its harsh treatment. "Damn." Courtney swore quietly, pressing her hands palm down on the kitchen counter as if she could physically push her temper back into place. "Damn, damn, damn!"

She looked around the kitchen countertops, searching for her cigarettes. She wanted a cigarette. Hell, she wasn't going to "dress the business up in comforting words"—she *needed* a cigarette!

There they were, next to the sink. She picked up the pack, shook one out and stuck it between her lips before reaching for matches. The matchbook was empty. "Damn!" she said around the cigarette.

She went down the length of the strange kitchen, opening and closing drawers, slamming cabinet doors, determined to find another matchbook. "Two months! Two lousy months—and ten days. I should congratulate her—the kid's set a new record."

She grabbed hold of a saltshaker and held it high in the air. "To Sydney Marie Blackmun, for having been thrown out of three private schools in less than two years, we would like to present our highest award—a bronzed discipline slip with gold-leaf cluster!"

She slammed the saltshaker down on the countertop, banged the last drawer shut, then whirled about to glare at the electric stove. "Any port in a storm," she told herself, reaching to turn on the front burner just as she heard the unmistakable sound of a lighter flicking to life behind her.

Obviously she was not alone.

She turned automatically and bent to put the cigarette tip to the flame, then stood back, inhaling the nicotine deeply. She exhaled in a rush, staring through the blue-gray haze at Adam Richardson, who had somehow found his way into her kitchen and then watched as she'd made a complete fool of herself. "Thank you," she said evenly. "Enjoy the show?"

"Not especially," he answered just as calmly, slipping the silver lighter back into his pants pocket. "You shouldn't smoke those things, you know. They'll kill you."

Courtney inhaled again, and exhaled through her

nose, feeling like an angry bull snorting a warning at an approaching matador. "Oh, goody," she said, smiling her meanest smile. "Just what I needed. A target. I'm ready to explode and I advise you to get out of my line of fire. Trust me in this, Adam—I'm not in the mood for a do-gooder sermon."

"Sorry, Courtney," Adam apologized. "I'll leave the warnings to the medical community."

"Oh, don't stop there, Adam. Lord knows, nobody else does. Everybody's an expert these days, and everybody has an opinion. Why don't you tell me I'm putting you in danger with my side-stream smoke?"

"And give you a reason to show me the door and a beach full of clean air?" he asked, leaning back against the kitchen counter. "Not on your life. Besides, I thought you might want directions to the Ninth Street bus station."

"You don't miss a lot, do you?" She did an about-face, turning on the faucet and holding the cigarette beneath the cold water, silently telling herself that she wasn't putting it out because of him. When she turned back he was still there, and he was still smiling.

Why didn't he go away? Couldn't he see that she was hanging on to her composure by her fingernails? She needed time alone, time to think, before Sydney arrived. *Sydney.* He knew about Sydney now—he had picked up on the bus station fast enough, hadn't he? Exactly how much had he heard? How much had she revealed in her telephone conversation and during her stupid tirade?

"So, how old is Sydney? I won't be swarmy and

say that you don't look old enough to have a daughter away at boarding school, but she can't be any more than ten or eleven.''

"She's thirteen,'' Courtney heard herself saying, although for the life of her she couldn't understand why she was bothering to answer his question. "Going on thirty.''

Adam laughed, as she had known he would. Turning around to face him, she looked into his eyes, expecting to see amusement and the usual curiosity. What she saw was concern and a hint of sympathy. Just what she always did her best to avoid!

Courtney rushed into speech. "Adam, I really don't want to be rude, but—''

"But don't let the door hit you on the tail on your way out?'' he offered as she floundered into silence.

She spread her arms wide. "That about covers it. I couldn't have put it better myself. The sloppy joe was good, and I appreciated the lunch, but I don't intend to let you blackmail me with it.''

Adam started for the door but stopped just as Courtney was about to let out a sigh of relief. "Look, Courtney, I don't mean to pry, really I don't but, well, maybe it would help to talk about it.''

She wrapped her arms tightly around herself at the waist. "No. It wouldn't. But thanks for the offer. This is between Sydney and myself. All I have to do is calm down between now and nine o'clock so that I don't give in to the urge to murder the kid.''

He scratched at a spot slightly above his left ear, smiling wryly. "I was kicked out of school once,

Courtney, just like your Sydney. My dad nearly had my hide for a hat rack. Poor guy, I really gave him fits for a few years. He never did figure out that all I really wanted was to be at home—with him."

Courtney sighed, realizing at last that Adam wasn't prying. He was being a friend. "Sydney loves boarding school. As a matter of fact, she's never seen a boarding school she didn't like. Her only problem is that they don't seem to like her." Maybe it would do her good to talk about it. "Why don't you go into the dining room, Adam, and I'll get us some coffee and that piece of cake I offered you just before I found out that Hurricane Sydney has struck again."

She poured two cups of coffee from the pot she'd left simmering, cut two slices of cake, and joined Adam in the dining room.

"This isn't going to do my cholesterol level any good, is it?" Adam asked, eyeing the gooey cake a moment before using his fork to break off a fluffy bite-size piece. "Sydney. I like that name. It's unusual. She's an only child?"

Courtney swallowed a piece of cake, feeling it head straight for her hips, and nodded. "That's one of the reasons she likes boarding school. Sydney has always made friends easily. You'd really like her, Adam," she said, suddenly anxious to make him understand that her daughter wasn't the holy terror Mrs. Breckenridge seemed to think she was. "She's a great kid."

"She'd have to be," he said, smiling at her. "You're her mother, aren't you?"

"I'm not sure which of us is the mother," Courtney

answered, reaching for her cup. Suddenly she wanted to tell Adam everything—everything she had kept so carefully hidden from the press. "I was only nineteen when she was born. Rob, my husband, died when she was only nine months old, and we sort of grew up together. I was orphaned at eleven and grew up in foster homes, so I had no family around to help me. As a matter of fact, there are times when I think Sydney's raising me. Lord, but she's smart. Public school didn't move fast enough to hold her interest. She'll probably grow up to be the first woman president—or Public Enemy Number One. Right now I think it could go either way."

"Incorrigible," Adam said. "I didn't mean to eavesdrop while you and Mrs. Breckenridge were talking, but I think I heard that word mentioned in passing."

"She's not going to put it on Sydney's record. The woman still likes her, even if Sydney did run Miss Hardcastle's undies up the flagpole to see if anyone would salute."

Adam's laughter was contagious, and before she knew it Courtney was laughing along with him. She felt as if she was part of a couple, the two of them chuckling over the exploits of their offspring. It was a good warm feeling.

Now from what part of left field could that unwanted thought have sprung? She and Adam weren't a couple. Far from it! They were two very separate people with absolutely nothing in common except the wall that separated their condos, and they wouldn't even have that much in common before too long. Not only that, but the last thing she wanted right now—needed right now—was to involve herself with a man. Especially a man like Adam, whose background and outlook on life was completely incompatible with hers.

Without warning, without rhyme or reason, Courtney's laughter threatened to turn to tears. She jumped up from the table and made a great business of carrying her plate and cup back into the kitchen before Adam could see her face.

But he *had* seen it. It was becoming increasingly apparent that Adam Richardson could see right through her.

She got as far as the sink when Adam put a hand on her wrist, sending a strange shiver up the length of her arm. "Courtney," he began softly, "I'm so sorry. I didn't mean to upset you, to bring up old hurts—about your husband and all. Please forgive me."

Courtney blinked back treacherous tears, setting her jaw as she allowed herself to take the out Adam had given her. If he wanted to think she was crying over Rob, or her past, she wasn't going to disabuse him of the notion. "Apology accepted. If you'll forgive me, as well. I don't know what got into me. I haven't spoken of Rob in years, not with anyone except Sydney. I must be more strung out than I thought."

She made a feeble attempt at lightening the atmosphere. "It has to be that, for Lord knows it can't be Sydney. After three schools in two years, I'm resigned to the fact that my daughter is destined to be thrown out of her schools faster than she can grow out of the uniforms.''

She could feel his thumb lightly stroking the soft inside of her wrist, sending her pulse pounding. "I'm flattered that you talked to me," Adam replied, still not releasing her. "I'll let you alone now to get ready for Sydney. You probably have to rehearse your mother-to-daughter speech. I know my dad had a real zinger for every occasion. But, please, Courtney, if you ever need to talk to somebody..."

Courtney was strong, and life had taught her to take almost anything on the chin without flinching. Anything, that was, except sympathy, or a comforting touch. The urge to collapse against Adam's broad shoulders and let him take on all her problems was almost overwhelming. And she couldn't let that happen.

Her self-control near the breaking point, she went on the defensive. She had been right to fear Adam's advent into her life. She pulled free of his grasp. "Thanks, Adam, but no thanks. Don't let these stupid tears fool you. If I've learned nothing else in the past thirteen years, I've learned one thing. Sydney is all that is important to me. Sydney, and my work. I don't need anything else, Adam. And I don't need—or want—any*body* else!''

The next thing Courtney knew, she was crushed against Adam's chest, and his mouth was warm and firm against hers. His arms were wrapped around her tightly, but not demandingly. He was giving, not taking, and his gift was the final telling blow to her composure. She lifted her arms to grasp him tightly, holding on to the rock-hard steadiness of him, the secure comfort of his strength, the haven of his encircling arms.

Courtney could feel herself responding, old memories coming to the surface in a rush of passion she had thought long buried. She allowed her mouth to soften beneath his, inviting him inside her own warmth, so that their tongues fought a silent duel that had no winner, no loser.

She was floating free, abandoning herself to the moment, to the need to hold on to somebody, taking strength from someone other than herself, with all thoughts of Sydney, of her writer's block, of her problems and priorities, blown to the winds.

How long they remained locked together she didn't know, but suddenly she was free, and Adam was smiling down at her, his strange gray eyes twinkling with gentle amusement. "We all need somebody, Courtney," he said before kissing her again, a short friendly kiss that landed somewhere on her left cheek. "I'll be right next door if you need me."

And then he was gone, leaving her to stand alone in the middle of Suzi's too-modern condo, one hand to her lips, tracing the invisible imprint of his mouth.

Chapter Four

"**B**or—ing." Sydney sighed lustily, pushing back the vertical blinds with one hand to look out over the deck of the condo and the dreary skies that wept into the slate-gray ocean. "I can't believe Suzi Harper talked you into this, Mom. Who in their right mind goes to the shore in, like, November?" she asked aloud, allowing the blinds to glide back into place. "It's, like, totally *devoid* of life."

"You, *like*, should have thought of that before lighting up in the little girl's room, bunkie," Courtney pointed out dispassionately as she walked into the living room and sat down on the couch to begin paging aimlessly through one of Suzi's endless supply of fashion magazines.

"Yeah, like, right," Sydney groused, slamming her slim, too-tall thirteen-year-old body onto a chair.

"You, *like*, picked up that particular annoying verbal habit at, *like*, Miss Potter's School for pubescent girls?" Courtney asked, reaching for a cigarette.

"Sure did," Sydney answered defensively, using her feet to move the swivel chair from side to side in a nervous jerky explosion of energy. "The same way I decided to try smoking from watching you. Not only did it get me expelled, it made me sick. Actually, Mom," she added facetiously, "now that I think about it, you should really be ashamed of yourself."

Courtney lit the cigarette, remembering Adam's reaction when she had lit one in his presence. "Spare me the public-service announcement—and the guilt trip, if you please, Sydney. I already gave at the office. And you know how I feel about smoking. I only smoke when I'm working, and soon maybe not even then if I can help it."

Sydney jumped up from the chair and approached the couch. "Baloney. I've been here for three days and you haven't worked yet. You're just hooked, admit it. I did a paper on it for science class. You're hooked all right—mentally and physically."

Courtney looked up at her daughter, then down at the smoking cigarette, and finally at the overflowing ashtray on the coffee table. Reaching forward, she crushed the cigarette into the crowded crystal dish. "When you're right, you're right, kiddo," she admitted on a sigh. "Why don't you open a couple of windows and we'll air out the place. I should only smoke in my office, anyway, as I do at home, so that you aren't exposed."

But Sydney didn't move to do as Courtney had suggested. She continued to stand in front of her mother, looking at her intensely. "What's up, Mom? I thought you came down here to write a book. When I was home for spring break you were writing so fast the computer was smoking almost as much as you."

Courtney heard the uncertainty in her daughter's voice and hastened to assure her that everything was fine. "The saga? That book is already in New York with Wilbur, to be released in April of next year. Now that I'm through with the tour on my last release, it's time to get back to work. It's just that this one is taking a little more preliminary work, that's all. Nothing to worry about, kiddo."

That lie out of her mouth, Courtney averted her eyes as she remembered a second lie she had told her daughter. When Sydney had asked her if she had met their next-door neighbor, "the one with the totally rad convertible," Courtney had told her that she had only met him once in passing. She reached for another cigarette.

Sydney reached across the coffee table to take the unlit cigarette from her mother's hand. "Can I help?"

Courtney looked up to see her daughter wearing her matronly too-old-for-her-years face. Damn her writer's block—and damn Adam Richardson. She had to get her act together before she scared Sydney. "Yes," she said brightly, "you sure can. This place is a shambles. How about helping me whip it back into shape before I make us some wickedly fattening lunch?"

"Oh, Mother," Sydney groaned, shaking her head. "That isn't what I meant, and you know it."

Courtney rose, picking up the ashtray and the morning newspaper as she headed for the kitchen. "Of course, I know it, my dear girl," she called over her shoulder. "But then I wouldn't be a mother, would I?"

Five minutes later, as Courtney was scrubbing celery for a tuna salad, Sydney walked into the kitchen, holding her mother's jacket in one hand.

"Honestly, Mom, and you say I'm a slob," she complained, motioning for her mother to move to one side so that she could throw something into the trash can. "Look at this," she commanded, holding out her hand. "You left your jacket on the chair and it felt lumpy when I picked it up. Your pockets were full of sand, and these stones!"

Courtney's hands stilled beneath the running water as she stared at the once brilliantly colored stones she had gathered on the beach the day she and Adam had shared lunch in his condo—the day he had kissed her and shaken her world to its very foundation. The stones were dry now, and all their lovely greens and blues and oranges had disappeared, so that now they were nothing more than anonymous brown rocks.

She had forgotten them and her intention to stand on the beach and watch the tide roll in, washing her sand-engraved name out to sea. Forgotten along with the stone and her name had been the wonderful carefree feeling that had inspired her to believe she had either the time or the inclination to engage in such lighthearted follies.

Lighthearted follies that had included Adam Richardson, the man she had not seen since that day but whose smiling face was always there, lurking in her subconscious, ready to assault her senses, her hard-won peace, each time she closed her eyes.

"Mom?" Sydney questioned, bringing Courtney back to her senses, to realize that she had been staring at the stones in mute fascination. "Are you sure you're all right? You wouldn't try to hide anything from me, would you? Like, if you're sick or something?"

Courtney quickly forced a bright reassuring smile onto her face. It wouldn't do to frighten Sydney. When there were only two of you, each was almost too important to the other person. "Of course I wouldn't do that, kiddo," she said lightly, deliberately turning her attention back to the now overly scrubbed, nearly shredded celery.

"Mom," Sydney whined, "don't patronize me. I'm not a child. If there's something wrong, you have to tell me."

Shutting off the water, Courtney turned back to her daughter. "All right," she said, sighing theatrically. "I'll come clean. I wasn't going to tell you this, Syd, but you're just too smart for me. I can't seem to get anything past you anymore."

Sydney looked at her mother intently, tilting her head to one side as if gauging Courtney's sincerity. "Go on," she said tentatively.

Courtney inclined her head toward the stones Sydney still held in her hand. "Those aren't really stones. They only *look* like stones. They're actually my marbles. Syd, you have to be brave. Your mother is losing her marbles!''

Sydney rolled her eyes. "Yeah, like, right," she said, just as Courtney leaned over to kiss her daughter on the cheek.

"You asked for it, sweetcakes," Courtney reminded her, giving Sydney an affectionate hug. A possible problem had been defused, with no harm done. Now, if she could only deal with her strange feelings for Adam so easily.

A person could walk along the same stretch of beach just so long before that person began to question his own sanity, or so Adam thought as he made his way back from the two-and-a-half-mile-long board-walk that still fell nearly a dozen blocks short of reaching Beatrice's condo.

The change of scene he had found on the boardwalk hadn't really helped, as most of the small stores had already been boarded up for the winter, including his favorite pizza shop.

It was strange. He had been walking on the beach every day for the five days he had been in Ocean City before Courtney Blackmun became his reluctant next-door neighbor, and had gloried in each private relaxed moment.

The quiet, the solitude, had given him the chance to unwind, to move, act and react without worrying whether or not it would make up a fifteen-second "sound bite" on the evening news. But now he hated the solitude and longed for someone to talk to.

"But not just any someone," he said out loud, knowing no one would hear him. "Just a certain green-eyed someone who wants me around about as much as a long-haired dog wants burrs."

He had heard her go out a few night ago to meet her daughter at the bus station, and had heard two car doors slam closed in the driveway an hour later. And that was the last he had heard of either Courtney or daughter Sydney.

They had been holed up in the condo ever since, surfacing neither for food nor for exercise. He knew. He had been watching and listening, knowing he was being stupid, but unable to put a halt to his ridiculous vigil.

Head down, ignoring the incoming tide, he walked along aimlessly, intent on his thoughts. Why had he kissed her? In retrospect, it had been a bad move, although it had seemed gloriously right at the time. She had even given in to him at first, given in with a sort of desperate hunger, but it hadn't lasted. He could see the withdrawal in her eyes as the kiss had ended, even as her hands had lingered, clutched against his back, the heat of her burning through his shirt to singe his skin.

Adam had known a lot of women, but he couldn't remember any of them affecting him as Courtney had done, right from the moment of their first explosive meeting, when he had realized that she didn't know who he was. And of course he had wanted to kiss her, so that when the opportunity had presented itself he had reached for it with both hands. Courtney Black-

mun was a vibrant beautiful woman, and he appreciated vibrant beautiful women.

But it was more than that. Courtney appealed to him
in every way, from her bright mind, to her caustic wit,
to the air of competence that couldn't quite disguise
her femininity, her vulnerability.

Beatrice had told him everything she knew about
Courtney, gleaned, he supposed, from his assistant's
endless files and steel-trap mind. It hadn't been much,
and focused mostly on Courtney's brilliant handling
of talk-show hosts and her ice-maiden image. Courtney Blackmun was a fine writer, which was public
knowledge, but she was a very private person. Beatrice
hadn't even known of Sydney's existence.

Beatrice wouldn't have believed him if he had told
her that it had been Courtney's supposedly nonexistent
vulnerability that had first attracted him to her, the
softness beneath the polished veneer of sophistication
that she wore so well for everyone, it seemed, except
him.

Of course, to take it one step further, Beatrice would
also have laid him out in lavender if he had told her
how he had then taken advantage of that vulnerability.
His action hadn't reflected well on his Boy Scout image, although it had probably gone a long way in re-
inforcing Courtney's opinion of him as a parasite who
lived for the moment. No, he shouldn't have kissed
her. Now she was back inside her protective shell, and
he didn't know how to get her out of it again.

Adam's hands clenched deep in the pockets of his
windbreaker as he remembered the pain in her eyes

when she had spoken of her childhood, a short emotional outburst he was sure Courtney had regretted the moment she had realized how much of her inner self she had been revealing to a near stranger.

At that moment he had wanted nothing more than to fold her in his arms and promise that she would never be alone again. As a matter of fact, if he didn't know better, he'd think he might be in danger of falling in love with the woman.

"Eligible Adam Richardson drooling over publishing's darling," Adam announced with a self-deprecating grimace, waving a hand in front of him as if picturing the words in a headline three inches high. How the tabloids would have loved it. He was acting like a lovesick teenager, for crying out loud, he groaned to himself, and over a woman who thought he was a monied beach bum. Maybe it was time he called Beatrice and told her he was going to fold his tent and come home.

"Hi. You, like, lost or something?"

Adam's head jerked to the right in surprise, giving him his first sight of Sydney Blackmun, who was perched on top of one of the huge metal drainpipes that was used to spill Ocean City street water runoff into the ocean. It had to be Sydney, he told himself, because she looked just like her mother must have looked before the rough edges of adolescence had been smoothed away.

He watched as Sydney hopped down from her perch, a tall slender girl with nearly waist-length straight black hair, which was being whipped across her pale pinched face by the wind coming off the ocean.

She was wearing a pair of worn-out sneakers, an oversize gray sweatshirt with a picture of Einstein on it and the words *Brains Are a Turn-on* and a pair of faded black jeans that must be making her circulatory system work overtime trying to pump blood to her lower limbs.

Along with her outfit, he noticed, she was wearing an eager in-love-with-the-world-and-everything-in-it expression that, even though their generations were different, reminded Adam very much of himself at Sydney's age.

He shook his head. "No, I'm not lost. You must be Sydney—better known as the Terror of Miss Potter's School. I'm Adam. Adam Richardson, your next-door neighbor. Perhaps your mother has mentioned me?" Did he sound too eager, he asked himself as he tried to appear casual. He kept his hands buried in his pockets, so as not to scare Sydney off.

"No-o-o," Sydney said, drawing out the word as she inspected Adam as if for flaws. "No, she hasn't. Sorry. That probably means she's deliberately forgotten she met you. She does that with people she, like, wants to avoid. She's developed it into an art form actually." Sydney took two more steps in Adam's direction. "Although I can't imagine her ever wanting to avoid *you*. Maybe I was right the first time, and she is sick."

"Sick?" Adam was all attention now, his fascination with the close physical resemblance between mother and daughter broken by Sydney's assumption. "Is she running a fever? Have you called a doctor? I was wondering why you haven't been out. Damn it, why didn't she let me know?"

Sydney laughed, waving her hands in dismissal. "Hey, take it easy. She's not that kind of sick, Mr. Richardson." She tapped the index finger of her right hand against her temple. "I mean *this* kind of sick. And not *really* sick, like she's hearing voices from outer space telling her to wrap herself in silver foil or anything. It's just that she isn't working, or sleeping very well, either, even if she is taking a nap this afternoon, which is why I'm out here, taking a look around. Mostly she's just kind of moping, and smoking like a chimney. Hey," she said, tipping her head to one side as she looked at him questioningly, "why am I telling you all this? You're not a reporter, are you? Mom would, like, *kill* me if you're a reporter."

Even her eyes were that same compelling emerald green, Adam thought.

"No," he assured her quickly as she seemed about to bolt, "I'm not a reporter. As I said, I'm your neighbor. I'm staying in the condo attached to yours. Your mother and I had just had lunch when the call came from Mrs. Breckenridge telling your mother you had gotten the boot from Miss Potter's. Maybe that's what's wrong with Court—your mother. Maybe she's depressed over her daughter being expelled from school?"

Sydney dismissed that idea with a toss of her long black hair. "Nah, I doubt it. After all, it's not like it's the first time. This makes three schools—two last year and one this year. She's getting, like, used to it by now."

She leaned closer to Adam, as if confiding some deep dark secret. "I think it's the book," she imparted knowingly. "It isn't going well. I overheard her yelling at Harry last night on the phone. Harry's really giving her grief. I'm playing dumb for now, pretending to believe her lies, but I'll find out what's going on sooner or later. I always do."

Adam felt his ears prick up, just like a hunting dog that has caught the scent of his quarry. "Harry?"

"Harry Gilchrist. Her agent," Sydney supplied helpfully. "She's told you about him, of course. Harry can be a royal pain in the— Well, anyway, he's really pushing at her for this book. *Questions of the Heart*, I think she calls it. She's supposedly been working on it since my summer vacation. *Sure* she is."

"I imagine you have a point to make," Adam quipped as Sydney made a face.

She leaned closer to him, her voice lowered for emphasis. "Early this morning I sneaked into the room she's using for her office and slipped the disk into the computer. Are you ready for this? It was empty. The start-up date for the disk was listed on the file as June, and the last time it was modified—or worked on—was yesterday. Six months, and the disk is still blank."

"I take it that's not good."

"Not good? It doesn't take the deductive reasoning of a Sherlock Holmes to figure out that something's very, very wrong. I think she's blocked. I've read about writer's block, and it can be deadly to someone like Mom, who positively *lives* to work. I think I'm going to suggest she have an affair or something—to take her mind off her problems. That, and make a phone call to that miserable Harry so that he gets off her back.''

For all his concern about Courtney, Adam could barely hide a smile as he thought about one major difference between mother and daughter. While Courtney never gave an inch, Sydney seemed unable to spill family secrets fast enough. Obviously his ''trustworthy'' face worked with at least one of the Blackmun women. ''Harry seems like such a slave driver,'' he put in, thinking he should contribute something more than the odd monosyllable to the conversation.

''He's just worried about being able to afford all the silk suits Mom's money has bought him,'' Sydney answered, bending down to pick up a small broken seashell and fling it toward the ocean. ''He's such a drag,'' she said, turning back to face Adam after the shell landed a disappointing fifteen feet from the water. ''One week this summer, when Mom was out west somewhere to do a talk show, he *grounded* me, just as if I was a *child*! As if it's *his* place to discipline me. I mean, who does he think he is—my father? Mom oughta dump him.''

Adam decided he did not like Courtney's literary agent, even if the little he knew about Sydney told him that she had probably deserved to be grounded. He'd had no right to punish the kid. As a matter of fact, if Sydney wanted to start a dump-Harry club,

Adam knew he would like to be a charter member.
Not that he was jealous of the man's relationship with
Courtney. Or was he? "Have you told your mother?"
he asked, his jaws tight.

Sydney dug the toe of her right sneaker into the hard
sand, avoiding his eyes. "I've thought about it," she
said quietly. "It's just, like, well, Mom seems to think
the sun rises and sets on the man."

"I see," Adam answered, although he didn't see at
all. If Harry was only Courtney's agent, why would
he be in charge of Sydney when Courtney was out of
town? How much of their association was business—
and how much was pleasure? He was beginning to see
Sydney through a green haze of jealousy. "Does your
mother date other men?" he asked, knowing he was
way out of line asking such personal questions. He
promised himself it would be the last one, but he had
to have an answer!

"*Other* men? You mean, besides Harry?" Sydney
laughed out loud. "I'd scarcely call Harry a *date*,
Adam—may I call you Adam? But yeah, she goes out
once in a while. She's too busy most of the time. But
you said you had lunch with her, didn't you? That
sounds like a date to me."

"Only a small one," Adam said, falling into step
beside Sydney as the girl began walking along the
beach toward the condo. Suddenly an idea bordering
on inspiration hit him. "Although she *did* give me a
rain check on dinner the other day. Would you care
to join us, Sydney? I'll make reservations for eight

o'clock tonight at a restaurant I discovered a couple of days ago. They make a mean plate of spaghetti."

"And garlic bread?" Sydney asked, dancing slightly ahead of him. "I'm so sick of school food. Honestly, they put American cheese and ketchup on bread and call it pizza. But when I sent out for two dozen pizzas late one night for the girls, you would have thought I'd committed a mortal sin. Headmistresses should have better nerves, don't you think?"

Adam laughed. "We'll have all the garlic bread you can eat," he assured her as she stopped at the bottom of the steps leading up to the deck. "There's only one small problem."

"Mother," Sydney declared knowingly, pulling a face. "She's being a wet blanket, right? Don't worry about it. *I'll* take care of her, Adam. You just be out front tonight at quarter to eight. We'll be there!"

Adam smiled as he climbed the stairs to his own deck, unable to explain his confidence in Sydney's powers of persuasion, but sure that she would deliver Courtney as promised. The smile faded as he entered his condo and spied the phone sitting on the coffee table.

Without bothering to take the time to remove his windbreaker, he picked up the receiver and pushed the automatic call button. "Beatrice?" he said a few moments later. "Write down this name. Gilchrist. Harry Gilchrist, a literary agent, probably working out of Manhattan. Got it? Okay, now get to work. I want it all—yesterday. What? I *am* resting, Beatrice. Everybody relaxes in his own way. Yeah, yeah. Thanks, sweetheart—I love you, too.''

Sydney was out of the miniscule back seat of the sports car and heading for the front door of the condo before Courtney fully realized what was happening. She looked like a gangly young colt, with her long hair flying out behind her. "'Night, Adam," the girl called back over her shoulder. "It was a terrific dinner—thanks again. Mom, take your time. I'll be in the shower, and you know how long I stay in the shower. Like, forever!"

Courtney turned to look at Adam, his profile highlighted by the double pair of lights suspended over the driveway. He wasn't actually smiling, but she was sure she could see the laugh lines around his eyes crinkle.

"Subtle, isn't she?" she asked, leaning her head back against the soft leather bucket seat, her stomach comfortably full, her instincts of self-protection slightly dulled by the wine she had drunk with dinner and her enjoyment of the evening.

"I think she's cute," Adam answered, removing the key from the ignition but making no move to open his car door.

"Of course, you do," Courtney said tongue in cheek. "Syd wouldn't have it any other way."

"A first-class conniver, huh?" Adam asked. "You never did tell me how she got you to agree to dinner."

She had to be careful how she handled this. It wouldn't do to have him know that not only did she not fight Sydney on the invitation, but she had spent an hour holed up in her bathroom, primping for the evening in a way she hadn't done in a long, long time.

"'Got me to agree?' Just what do you mean by that?" Courtney countered, deliberately pretending not to understand what he meant. "It wasn't any big deal. You were just collecting on the rain check you asked me for the other day. Besides, after four days in that condo with Sydney and her music collection—and I call that god-awful noise music only to be charitable— I was so stir-crazy I would have accepted an offer from King Kong to share a bunch of bananas on top of the Empire State Building while we watched the airplanes coming in for the kill."

She watched as Adam seemed to mentally prepare an explanation before he said finally, "Just forget I mentioned anything, Courtney. I guess I overreacted the other day. After all, it was only one kiss."

"Two actually," Courtney reminded him, wondering why she was being so direct. "You forgot the one on my cheek."

Now Adam smiled, his teeth very white in the darkness, and her heart did a little flip in her chest. Oh, yes, this man did have a way of getting to her.

"You counted, huh?" he teased, easing himself closer to her, with only the console separating their two relaxed bodies. "I think I'm flattered."

Courtney felt her muscles tensing in reaction. "Yes, well, just don't let it go to your head," she warned, although whether she was warning him or herself she wasn't sure. Why did he have to be so darned appealing? Sydney was already more than halfway in love with the guy, and she, well, Courtney didn't exactly know how she felt about Adam Richardson. She just knew that indifferent didn't cover it.

Her eyes closed and warning bells went off in her head as Courtney felt his arm find its way across the back of her seat, but she didn't move away. It wasn't as if she was an impressionable immature teenager who was in danger of getting in over her head. She was thirty-three years old, for crying out loud—certainly old enough to know what she was doing!

She tried to remember the last time she had been kissed in a car. A small sad smile curved the corners of her mouth when she realized that it had been a long time ago—a lifetime ago. It had been Rob, sweet loving Rob, her husband, who had introduced her to the delights to be found in the time-honored custom called necking.

But, she remembered as she felt Adam's fingertips lightly stroking the soft skin behind her left ear, sending tingles of pleasure running down her spine, Rob had never been so smooth, had never dared to act with such assurance of his own sensual prowess, even after their marriage. He had been young—fumbling, nervous and clumsy. Adam was a lot of things, but clumsy wasn't one of them. And he was a man, Courtney reminded herself, where Rob, no matter how loving, had been a boy.

Rob, the boy, had loved her and wanted her. Adam, the man, was attracted to her and had—as men were so apt to point out—needs. As she allowed her head to tip to the right, wordlessly giving Adam's warm lips access to her slim throat, Courtney tried desperately to remember that fact.

And that wouldn't be difficult to do. After all, she had needs too, didn't she? She felt them now, uncurling somewhere deep inside her, and realized that she had not, as she had believed at the time, buried those needs along with Rob.

"Courtney?" Her name, a whispered caress against her earlobe, was less a plea than a question.

"Hmm?" she responded, wondering how a nice girl like her had come to be in a situation like this. It was alien to everything in her. Her entire reaction to Adam was totally unrelated to anything she had ever experienced and—she forced herself to remember—she thoroughly detested his aimless pleasure-oriented existence even as she was attracted to him.

"Tell me about Harry Gilchrist."

Adam's question hit her with the numbing shock of a bucketful of ice water flung smack into her face. The mood was shattered, gone before she had been able to truly convince herself that it had existed at all. She sat forward, her shoulder-length hair swirling around her face like an ebony curtain as she whirled around to confront Adam, her eyes open wide as she stared at him in confusion.

"What? What do you mean, 'Tell me about Harry Gilchrist'? How did you learn about—Sydney! She was listening! Military school, my sweet patoot! Mrs. Breckenridge didn't go far enough. What that kid needs is a good dose of boot camp!"

She turned away to fumble with the door handle, a

recessed semicircle of metal whose function at the moment eluded her. "Damn this stupid contraption! And damn you, Adam Richardson!" she exclaimed as the door finally jerked open. "You sure do know how to ruin an evening!"

Her high heels had just made contact with the cement driveway when Adam's hand snaked out to roughly pull her back against the seat.

"Calm down," he ordered in a cold official-sounding voice, using both of his strong hands to pin her against the soft leather seat. "It's not going to do you or Sydney a bit of good if you go shooting into the house like a runaway rocket. The kid's worried about you. I think she believes Harry has something to do with your inability to write."

She tried to free her arms. "So she came crying to you? Who are you, anyway? Her father confessor—or some sort of magician, weaving spells around women so that they tell you everything you have no right to know? What's the matter, Adam? Are you so bored with your jet-set life that you've taken up cocktail-party psychoanalysis? First Sydney and now me. Give me a break!"

Just as quickly as her temper flared, it cooled, as realization of all that Adam had said sunk into her brain. Sydney *knew*. She knew about Harry—although she could only be guessing. She couldn't know all of it. And Sydney also knew about her writer's block. After she had tried so hard to protect her, to shield Sydney from her problems! Courtney sagged against the seat, all the fight going out of her. "Oh, God,

Adam," she breathed on a sob. "She knows. Sydney knows."

Courtney felt Adam's arms close around her and did not pull away. This was the last thing she wanted, but desperately needed. This was not like her, to lean on somebody else, yet she felt so right.

She could hear his voice, murmuring softly, filling her head with nonsense words of sympathy, and instead of anger she felt gratitude. Gratitude and the unexplainable feeling that, of all the people in the world, this one man, this one very unusual, very extraordinary man, was capable of understanding all the secrets of her heart.

"I'm not going to cry," she said, more to convince herself than him. "I never cry."

She could feel his fingers tangling through her hair at the nape of her neck, his gentle caress urging her to lean on him, encouraging her to borrow some of his strength, inviting her to accept his comfort.

"Everybody cries sometime. Maybe it's time you did. Bend a little, Courtney," he whispered hoarsely. "Strong people have to learn how to bend, like trees in the wind, or else one day they'll break."

Her voice catching on a sob, Courtney buried her head against his chest and let the storm come at last.

Chapter Five

Courtney sat huddled in a corner on the delicate sofa, her stockinged feet tucked beneath her, a small gold-and-white-striped satin throw pillow clutched against her chest, watching as tongues of flame caught at the logs in the fireplace, lending the only light to the otherwise dark room.

She thought about her cigarettes, sitting in her purse on the coffee table, thought about them in the way she was sure an alcoholic would think about a drink—longingly, as if having one, just one, would help—but she didn't reach for the pack.

The song floating from the stereo was an old 1940s' standard telling the sort of soft hypnotic musical story that warned against the pitfalls of love while at the same time seducing the listener into believing that love was the only fate worth pursuing.

Her eyes were puffy, she was sure of it, as she had

never been a graceful crier. Her nose always ran, and she had the exasperating habit of developing a very loud case of hiccups every time she let her emotions get the best of her.

This last bout of tears, her first real emotional release in more years than she could remember, had run the whole gamut of messiness. Her eyes burned, her chest hurt and she was still unable to stifle the random sobs. All in all, Courtney did not feel particularly glamorous or seductive. She barely felt human.

How she always envied the graceful crier, the sort of woman who could, almost on demand, produce glistening eyes, a pouting mouth, and a single enormous heart-wrenching tear that glided caressingly down one adorably flushed cheek, melting the hearts of everyone around her.

These were the same women who blossomed in frigid weather, walking across a snowy expanse, eyes shining, lips and cheeks rosy red, and looking more appealing than a Norman Rockwell painting. She, on the other hand, turned pale as marble when exposed to wind and cold.

"Come to think of it, my nose runs then, too," she said out loud, addressing the flames in the fireplace.

"Want another tissue?" Adam asked, walking into the living room. "Here, take this coffee while I check the bathroom. Beatrice is bound to have a box someplace."

Courtney looked up to see Adam standing in front of her, a steaming coffee mug in his hand. He was no more than a blur really, his tall frame lighted from the back by the fire and the small spill of light coming from the kitchen.

Comfortingly faceless, momentarily not Adam Richardson, *man,* but just the sexless supportive figure on whom she had dissolved into a weeping puddle, she still found it amazingly easy to talk to him. "I think the waterworks have shut off at last, thank goodness," she said, shaking her head. "But I will take that coffee. It smells delicious."

She wrapped her cold hands around the oversize mug, closing her eyes as she took several small bracing sips of the hot liquid, so that she felt rather than saw Adam sit down beside her on the sofa.

The coffee tasted good, almost too good. Turning to face him, she asked, "Special beans, Adam? Tell me, what proof are they? And what makes you think I need a drink? I never drink." Of course she didn't. She didn't like to lose control, and she had seen too many people abandon all their inhibitions after a few friendly drinks.

She saw the flash of his white teeth as he grinned. "It's just some brandy—only for medicinal purposes, of course. Do you mind?"

"No." Courtney shook her head, not really angry. How could she be angry? Hadn't she just gotten through blubbering all over his shoulder? What was he supposed to do—offer her some warm milk and a bracing sermon? "At the moment, Adam, I think it might be just what the doctor ordered. I don't know what came over me outside in the car. I can't even remember what you said that finally got through to me, but I really lost it there for a while. Please forgive me.''

Adam's hand reached out and she placed the coffee mug in it, then subsided against the cushions, the throw pillow now lying forgotten in her lap. She felt the brandy create a pleasant warmth in her stomach as every muscle in her body seemed to unclench and even coax her to relax. She wouldn't lose her control, but it would be nice to misplace it for a time.

"This is nice," she said, looking toward the fireplace. Courtney was secretly amazed at how right this all felt, how good *she* felt, just being with him. "Oh, look, Adam. There—in the flames. Doesn't that look like a medieval castle?''

Adam leaned forward, as if to see better, his left hand sitting familiarly on her shoulder. She liked the feeling. "A castle? Where? Oh, wait a minute, I see it now. It's a big one, isn't it? I like the turrets. And look—there's Sir Lancelot, riding up to the drawbridge.''

Courtney giggled, the lighthearted sound of her own laughter surprising her. "That's not Sir Lancelot, that's a dragon. He has come to destroy the castle and everyone in it. See the blue-white flames shooting out of his mouth? He's going to huff, and puff and—''

"Wrong fairy tale, Courtney," Adam interrupted, leaning back so that his arm now circled her shoulders. "The big bad wolf huffed and puffed, remember?''

Courtney did remember—remembered thinking those same words about Adam when she had seen him that first time. She felt a sly smile curving her lips as she looked at him through her lashes, knowing but not caring that the action could be viewed as seductive. "Oh, Adam, if you only knew—" she began, just as his mouth settled on hers, instantly igniting an inferno between them that would have incinerated Sir Lancelot, the dragon and the entire castle in half a heartbeat.

Courtney willingly melted against him, her legs uncurling from beneath her as Adam slipped backward, his arms wrapping around her, pulling her with him, until he lay on the soft cushions, Courtney's body fitting against his from chest to knee.

Everywhere their bodies touched, hungry sparks of fire pricked at her. Her body began to remember the heady feel of lovemaking and it softened expectantly, preparing itself for the delights that were sure to follow.

Courtney was in a fragrant garden of earthly pleasures, experiencing an ever-increasing sensation of warmth, of excitement, of need. Almost as though it was happening to someone else, she felt her burgundy silk blouse slide away, to be followed by the lacy wisp of pink lingerie that momentarily had barred the way to complete freedom.

Adam's hands moved expertly, instinctively searching out and capturing her soft breasts and then teasing them into flower beneath his hands. Courtney knew she was lost, powerless against him—powerless against her own desires, her own needs.

Her emotions, stretched to the breaking point and beyond, soaked up the solace of his passion like a dry sponge, losing its rough brittle texture as the sweet balm of Adam's ministrations soothed away all pain, all thought, all restraint.

She wanted to give herself to him. She wanted Adam to give himself to her. It didn't matter that they had nothing in common. It didn't matter that their backgrounds were as different as a high-priced department store was from a five-and-dime, that their views of the world came from opposing poles. There was no tomorrow for them, no future. But there *was* tonight—and tonight she needed what Adam seemed so willing to give.

But are you being fair? a small voice asked as Adam lifted her into his arms, only to gently lower her next to him on the plush carpet in front of the fire.

You're being greedy, the small voice accused as Courtney's trembling fingers undid Adam's tie, then worked their way down the row of buttons on his crisp white shirt, her lips tracing the path her fingers had taken.

This isn't like you, Courtney Blackmun, the voice pointed out rationally, still not ready to give up the fight. *You detest women who use people. You've held yourself aloof from this sort of thing. For thirteen years you've been above this, better than this.*

But I've been so lonely, so scared and lonely, Courtney countered silently, lying back, watching in fascination as Adam stretched out beside her, his strange gray eyes, their expression so gentle, so understanding, so giving, never leaving hers.

Courtney extended her arms, folding them around Adam's bare back as she buried her head against his chest. "So damned lonely," she whispered softly, hoping only her heart would hear.

Adam awoke on the floor, every muscle protesting as he rolled over onto his side, dragging along the handmade patchwork quilt Courtney had used to cover him.

What time was it, anyway? He squinted toward the small crystal clock that sat on the coffee table, vaguely making out the hour to be somewhere between ten and eleven in the morning.

"Don't look now, old man, but I think you missed the sunrise," he told himself, groaning as he got to his feet. He looked around, noticing first the deader-than-dead ashes in the fireplace, then spying his shirt, which had been tossed to one side without a thought as to how much silk rebelled at being treated like polyester.

Leaning down to pick up his shirt, he headed for the spiral staircase to the lower level and the shower stall in the bathroom off his bedroom. Fifteen minutes later he was dressed in navy cotton slacks and an ivory wool fisherman's sweater, sitting at the bar in Beatrice's blue-and-white-chintz kitchen, sipping coffee and remembering, in great fascinating detail, the events of the previous evening.

He started out slowly, deliberately recalling the dinner that Courtney, Sydney and he had shared at the local spaghetti house. It had been a pleasant meal, with Sydney taking on the lion's share of the conversation while he and Courtney had served as an amused audience, laughing in all the right places as Sydney told outrageous stories about Miss Potter's School.

It was only after he had pulled the sports car into the driveway that the evening had begun to get sticky. Sydney, bless her little matchmaking heart, had disappeared on cue, almost as if he had bribed her to do so, leaving him and Courtney alone in the dark car.

Adam had known the evening was going to end with a kiss, he remembered, realizing he might have been a trifle arrogant, but he'd had no idea of the explosion the mere mention of Harry Gilchrist's name was going to cause. That, and Courtney's realization that Sydney was aware her mother was having trouble writing her latest book.

Adam decided that, not being a parent himself, he couldn't fully understand how devastated Courtney had been to learn that she hadn't been able to protect her child from a reality she didn't wish her to know. He only knew that Courtney was, in his opinion, being optimistically unrealistic in trying to balance the entire world on her shoulders; by being mother, writer, unwilling celebrity and businesswoman.

But did he really see himself in the role of Courtney's helpmate? What had he been trying to do by forcing her into thinking about Sydney and Harry? Why did he feel as if Courtney Blackmun's problems were not only becoming his problems, but that he *wanted* them to be his problems.

Adam took his coffee cup with him into the living room, sat down on the sofa and rested his bare feet on the coffee table. His eyes strayed to the area carpet in front of the fireplace.

It was time to think about what had happened here, on the sofa, and there, as he and Courtney lay in front of the fire, the white-hot heat of their bodies making the warmth of the fire pale into insignificance.

She had been a wonder, a glory; shy, modest, yet endlessly giving, endlessly receptive. At first he had felt as nervous as he would have if she had been a virgin, for she had seemed unsure of exactly what he wanted, and even of what she wanted. But she *had* been married, had known at least one other man, and Adam had fought to remind himself of that as she had stopped placidly accepting his advances and begun making some tentative moves of her own.

Yet, as their passion had built, threatening to consume them, he had seen the fear, the growing uncertainty in her eyes, the first slight dawning of what they were doing—of what they were about to do. It had been enough to convince Adam to curb his passion and settle for holding her close until she had felt safe enough to fall asleep.

Oh, yeah, Adam told himself mockingly, *you were a real saint, weren't you? First you upset the woman, break down all her defenses, and then you start playing a two-bit Romeo, plying her with brandy and damn near seducing her. Don't look now, old man, but your Boy Scout image is sporting a black eye.*

"I don't know what's going on, but I've got the sinking feeling that this woman is going to change my life—if she ever lets me close to her again." Adam's jaw set, his hands gripping the coffee mug tightly, as he stared into the cold fireplace, his gray eyes steely with determination. "Maybe it's time Courtney and I sat down and exchanged some home truths."

It's the things we don't do that destroy us, not the things, right or wrong, that we have done. To err is human; to refuse to try is downright criminal.

Elliot, glaring into the steam-clouded mirror as he tried to position the small ragged square of rice paper over the bleeding cut on his chin, the bottom half of his face still covered with rapidly drying shaving soap, stopped what he was doing to consider what he believed to be the most profound thought he'd ever had before six in the morning, and most certainly the most profound thought he'd ever had sober.

He looked toward the chair in the corner and the pile of clothing that waited for him there: his funereal black slacks, vest, hat and silk shirt, his thin bowstring tie, a pair of five-hundred-dollar boots he'd won off a fool who had drawn on an inside straight in a poker game in San Antonio, and the double-holstered gun belt containing the two silver-handled pistols that never left his sight day or night.

He finished shaving, impatiently wiping the remaining flecks of soap from his face with a rough towel, hating the knowledge that a steady hand wouldn't have allowed a cut on his chin. Profound thoughts, it seemed, made him clumsy.

Courtney sat back in the chair, moving the mechanical mouse so that she could click once on the Save button, knowing that this time, this beginning, was the right one. *Questions of the Heart* was finally on its way. Elliot Marshall, her hero, was about to walk out of the two-bits-a-night hotel and into publishing history.

She read the passage again, savoring the heady feeling of accomplishment that flowed through her body.

"Damn, I'm good!" she said, sitting straight once more, her fingers flying over the keyboard as she took Elliot through the front door of the hotel and into the dusty streets of San Francisco to meet adventure and before too much longer, his fate.

"A blond five-foot-two fate named Melinda," she announced to the empty room two hours later, as Elliot's latest adversary lay writhing in pain in the dusty street, his hands clutched around his bullet-shattered kneecap, "and she's going to show him just what life is all about, poor boy."

"Mom? You talking to yourself again? Gosh, it's smoky in here. Mom—are you in there anywhere? Talk to me, Mom, so I can try to find you through this mess."

"Very funny, Syd. You ought to go on the night-club circuit with a comedy act like that," Courtney suggested, turning to look at her daughter before her attention went back to the computer screen.

Sydney entered the room, waving her hands in front of her as if trying to fight her way through the haze of cigarette smoke. "Hey—you're still in your clothes. You been up all night? You haven't done that in ages. I guess I fell asleep waiting for you to come in. Do you know it's almost eleven o'clock? I love sleeping late. Did you and Adam stay outside long?"

Without her fingers missing a beat on the keyboard, and without looking up, Courtney replied, "Almost, I know, no, and none of your business. Have you had breakfast yet, honeybunch?"

"Honeybunch? My, my, my. We *are* in a good mood this morning, aren't we?" Sydney moved across the room to stand behind her mother and look over her shoulder at the computer screen. "Page twenty-two?" She gave Courtney an affectionate slap on the back. "*All right, Mom!* I knew Adam would know just what to do to cheer you up."

Courtney could feel her cheeks reddening and purposely avoided turning around, knowing that Sydney would get entirely the wrong idea about her and Adam.

Actually, Courtney admitted to herself ruefully, Sydney would probably get exactly the right idea, and Courtney didn't believe she was "liberated" enough to want her thirteen-year-old daughter to know she had spent most of the night with a man, even if nothing had happened.

It had almost happened, and that was enough.

Besides, knowing Sydney, the girl would immediately start weaving daydreams about Adam, casting him in the role of father, and the three of them in the role of perfect family. Having a father and a mother— not to mention a house in the country with a white picket fence around it, and a dog and two cats—was Sydney's favorite fantasy. Courtney could understand that, for it had been a fantasy of hers, too, many, many years ago.

How could Courtney explain that she and Adam had spent the night together, that they had almost made love? *She and Adam had almost made love?* Courtney, with her writer's instincts, immediately caught the mental words she had used to describe what had almost taken place between herself and Adam last night and held them up in front of her mind's eye to examine them.

Almost made love. Were those the right words?

How else could she refer to what had happened between them? What else did she want to call it? How did she want to think of it? Courtney pressed her lips together as a wave of pleasure liberally mixed with pain coursed through her body. Yes, she decided fatalistically, they had almost made love—beautiful, wonderful love.

They had held each other, shared with each other, until Adam had called a halt by pulling her into his arms, her head on his shoulder as they had stared into the dying flames of the fireplace.

They must have fallen asleep, because it had been nearly dawn when Courtney had awakened, her body intimately curled against his. She had kissed Adam one last time as he lay on his back, his arms crossed behind his head, his eyes closed, a most wonderfully contented smile on his face, then had straightened her clothing and slipped out onto the deck.

Now it was eleven o'clock, and she had been in this room ever since she had run barefoot across the sand to her own condo, writing as fast as her fingers could follow her thoughts.

"Mom?" Sydney prompted, still standing behind her mother. "You in never-never land again? Gosh, I hated it when you weren't writing because you seemed so unhappy, but now I remember how much I hate it when you're on a roll. Now I'd bet I could come in here with my hair on fire and you wouldn't even notice. I guess I'd better go make you some lunch, or else you'll just starve to death down here hunched over your computer. It's already way too late for breakfast."

Courtney looked at the screen and the blinking cursor that waited so patiently for her to type in the next sentence. Her mind, which had been so full of ideas, so eager to work, seemed to have flipped a silent switch to Stun. She couldn't remember what she had written, and had no idea what was supposed to come next.

Who was her newly thought-of heroine? It started with an M, she was sure of that. Melissa? Melinda? Martha? She hit the Save button one more time, then shut the computer down.

"I'll take a shower while you're making lunch, Syd," she said, pushing herself away from the desk. "Then maybe we can take a walk together on the beach. A long walk. All right?"

Sydney was already heading for the door. "Awesome! Do you think Adam will want to come along? I could run over and ask him. He might sleep late, too, but I don't think he could sleep this long, do you?"

Courtney's right hand moved unconsciously to her blouse, the fingers convulsively closing around the lapels, bringing the top of the blouse close against her throat, as if to cover her sudden nakedness. "Adam? You want to ask Adam?" she repeated, knowing her voice sounded strained.

This was ridiculous. She was acting more like a village idiot than Chester Dingman. She wasn't afraid to see Adam again, was she? They were two adults; they had known what they were doing. After all, they hadn't been the first two people to succumb to a volatile situation, to a fleeting moment of passion. And, when you got right down to it, nothing had happened.

Well, that wasn't quite true. Something had happened. A *lot* of something. As a matter of fact, if it hadn't been for Adam's wonderful powers of restraint, *everything* would have happened. She certainly hadn't been in any condition to stop him.

Another man would have taken complete advantage of her confused emotional state, but Adam had been a gentleman. He had been there for her, allowed her to use him up to a point, and then had held her close against his warm bare chest all through the night, to keep away the demons of the dark. She owed him a lot.

At the very least, she owed him an invitation to walk with them along the beach.

"I—I don't see any reason why you shouldn't ask him, Syd. We could all walk down to the boardwalk and see if any of the cafés are open for lunch," she said at last, silently congratulating herself for being so calm. "I only say that because it's my turn to do the dishes."

It was later, as she stood beneath the steaming water of the glass-enclosed shower, as the soapy washcloth skimmed the length of her body, that she remembered all the reasons why seeing Adam again might be the biggest mistake of her life.

The sun winked off the waves benignly rippling toward the shore, while the light breeze coming off the land was warm rather than bracing. It was in fact one of those rare, perfect, balmy late-autumn days that never failed to set Beatrice off on an impassioned sermon about the "greenhouse effect," "global warming," and the urgency of banning all nuclear testing. But then, of course, anything was liable to set Beatrice off about nuclear testing. Adam adored Beatrice's passions, and he considered it a compliment when his detractors termed him passionate as well.

Passionate. He sneaked a covert glance at Courtney, who was walking on the other side of Sydney, her hands thrust deeply into the pockets of her emerald-green jeans, her dark head thrown back to watch the gulls that screeched above their heads as the three of them strolled slowly up the boardwalk.

Adam didn't know what he had expected when he had joined the two women on the beach an hour earlier, but he was darn sure he hadn't expected what he'd gotten. Sydney had been happy to be out and about on another "Ocean City adventure," as she termed it. The child was so vibrant, so achingly alive, that he had been hard-pressed not to grab her in a fatherly bear hug and share in her simple joy.

Courtney, however, had been another story.

She had been pleasant enough all through lunch at a small café located just off the boardwalk, he would grant her that, but it was a purely professional pleasantness, donned for the occasion, just as one donned a coat to go out into the cold—for protection.

She spoke, she walked, she smiled, but there were no secret looks passing between them, no silent acknowledgment of the closeness they had shared not all that many hours before in Beatrice's condo. It was only when he looked at her closely, when she stopped her overly ambitious examination of the scenery for a moment, that he could see a hint of the soft yielding woman he had held in his arms; a certain dewiness in her green eyes, a flattering blush to her perfect skin.

She had spent the remainder of the night and most of the morning working on her book. Sydney had told him that, presenting him with the knowledge as if the break in Courtney's writer's block had been a gift he had given and she was thanking him for it.

He smiled, remembering that Sydney had shared the credit with the dinner of spaghetti, meatballs and potent garlic bread, simplistically believing that her mother had just needed to get out for an evening, let her hair down, and the dam that had been holding back the torrent of words had broken.

Adam hadn't disabused Sydney of her conclusion.

But now he and Courtney were strangers again. Friendly strangers, but strangers just the same. Sydney was unwittingly acting as a buffer between them, and Adam was torn between being thankful for her presence and wishing her at the other end of the world.

He was glad Courtney was writing again and pleased that he had been responsible for inspiring her—if that was the word for it. But he was getting the most uncomfortable feeling that he was now superfluous, his continued presence unnecessary, and possibly even unwanted.

It wasn't a particularly pleasant feeling. He wasn't angry; Adam was conscious enough of his own participation in the events of the previous evening not to be angry with Courtney. After all, it hadn't been one-sided lovemaking, and she had not been the only one inspired by it.

"Look Adam—a bookstore," Sydney exclaimed, interrupting his depressing thoughts. "Let's go inside and see if they have any of Mom's books."

Adam watched as Courtney rolled her eyes in a comic display of dismay. Obviously this was not an unusual request on Sydney's part. Courtney's words confirmed his thoughts. "Only if you promise not to embarrass me by grabbing one of the books and yelling, 'My mom wrote this!' at the top of your lungs," she warned, tapping her daughter lightly on the tip of her nose.

After Sydney crossed her heart and solemnly promised to be a perfect angel they went into the small store, Adam holding open the door so that the two females could pass through in front of him. It took only a few moments to locate a shelf holding several paperback copies of three of Courtney's books.

Sydney picked one up and took it to the counter where a young bored-looking clerk stood, chewing an enormous wad of bubble gum that gave off an almost overpowering odor of tropical fruit. "I'd like to purchase this book, please," Sydney trilled sweetly as she dug a twenty-dollar bill out of her jeans pocket and plunked it on the counter. "I understand it's very, *very* good."

Courtney, standing in front of a display of local history books depicting the history of Ocean City and nearby Cape May, lowered her head, her back turned to her daughter.

"Okay, if you say so. I don't read," the clerk explained matter-of-factly. "I just work here." She blew a big orange bubble and, as Adam watched in admiring fascination, drew it back into her mouth before closing her lips around it, so that it exploded against her molars. "You got anything smaller?" she asked Sydney. "I can't break a twenty unless I go next door to the gift shop."

Adam picked up copies of Courtney's two other novels and laid them next to Sydney's choice. "Here, does this make it easier?" he asked, giving the clerk his "trust me" smile. "As this young girl says, they're supposed to be *very* good books."

The clerk shrugged. "Makes no matter to me how you spend your money," she said, bagging the books and then quickly making change for the twenty.

Behind them, Courtney laughed out loud.

Sydney looked up at Adam, and he could see Sydney's anger bubbling very close to the surface. It must be terrible to have a famous mother and not be able to crow about it once in a while, at least a little bit. Even worse, her mother was being very uncooperative. Courtney had even, he noticed, unearthed an enormous pair of very dark sunglasses and slipped them on, hiding her very recognizable emerald eyes.

Adam leaned slightly across the counter, using his thumb to point back over his shoulder. "You see that lady? The one over there, trying to look inconspicuous?" he asked the young clerk. "She *wrote* these books."

The clerk shifted the wad of gum to one side of her mouth as she tipped her head to look toward Courtney. "Sure," she said, obviously unimpressed, "and I'm Danielle Steel."

Adam's hand snaked out to grab Sydney's arm, as Sydney was beginning to show signs of becoming violent.

"No," he corrected the clerk, his smile still in place. He pointed once more to Courtney, who was in the process of heading for the safety of the boardwalk. He turned over one of the books to show the clerk Courtney's picture on the back cover. The clerk looked from the book, to Courtney, and then back to the cover once more. The wad of tropical-fruit bubble gum dropped to the counter as the clerk's eyes and mouth opened wide. "*She's* Courtney Blackmun," Adam announced triumphantly, "and *you're* not!"

The trio stumbled back onto the boardwalk, their

arms linked, laughing so hard tears came to their eyes. Sydney reached up first to Adam, then to Courtney, kissing their cheeks. "Oh, that was absolutely the greatest! Did you see her eyes? They nearly popped out of her head! I mean, it was, like, totally rad!"

Adam looked over the top of Sydney's head to see Courtney smiling at him, all the professionalism gone, all the ice melted, and the real Courtney exposed the way she had been last night. He thought his heart would explode in his chest. "Hi," he mouthed silently, so that Sydney wouldn't notice.

Courtney slipped the sunglasses down to the end of her nose, showing him the smile in her own eyes. "Hi, yourself," she mouthed back at him as they turned around and headed for home, three musketeers charging down the boardwalk, their feet hitting the boards in unison like marching soldiers returning home from a successful campaign.

It was only when they came to the steps leading up to the deck on Courtney's side of the condo that the mood was broken. For standing at the top of the stairs was a very petite, very beautiful blonde, both her glorious hair and her flamboyantly styled knee-length scarlet cloak blowing about in the wind.

"Courtney, you sneak, how do you do it?" the blonde called down the stairs. "I've come here every summer for three years, and I've never landed a fish like *him*!"

Chapter Six

"Adam, huh?" Suzi Harper repeated after the introductions had been made, looking at him closely as they sat across the dining-room table from each other, waiting for the coffee Courtney had promised them. "You know, you sure do look familiar. Do you have a last name?"

Adam winced inwardly. This could be sticky. He wanted Courtney to know who he really was—correct her unfavorable impression of him as a spoiled playboy taking a break from his jet-set life-style—but he had planned for the information to come out later, when they were alone.

"Richardson," he said at last, hoping his voice sounded nonchalant. "Adam Richardson." He hastened to add, "You said you live here at the beach in the summer, Suzi. I won a yachting race here this past summer, and my picture was in the local paper—stick-

ing out from behind the loving cup. I was the one with
the big ears.''

Suzi waved a blood-red-tipped hand dismissingly.
''No, that's not it. I don't read the newspapers—I read
entirely too much at work—or even watch the news
on television; they're both so depressing. Adam Richardson,'' she mused aloud, absently taking a steaming
mug of coffee from Courtney. ''Thank you, darling.
Oh, wait a minute—now I know!''

Adam closed his eyes. Suzi Harper knew. It was all
going to hit the fan now, and Courtney would never
forgive him for not leveling with her from the word
go.

''You remind me of a young Peter O'Toole!'' the
book reviewer exclaimed triumphantly, pointing one
red-enamel dagger at him. ''Oh, I know you're dark
and he's blond, and you really aren't built the same
or anything, but it's your eyes. You have the same sort
of long sexy bedroom eyes.'' She swiveled in her chair
to face Courtney. ''You agree with me, don't you,
darling? Hasn't Adam got the most sexy eyes?''

Sydney, who was sitting in the chair beside Suzi,
picked up a strand of her long dark hair and began
twirling it around her finger in a circular motion as
she pointed to her head. ''Isn't Suzi brilliant, Adam?''
she purred, as if humoring a certifiable tweety-bird.
''It's all so clear now. I just can't figure out how Mom
and I missed it. Did I ever tell you how much I loved
you in *Lawrence of Arabia*?''

''Put a lid on it, Syd,'' Courtney warned quietly as
she sat in the chair at the head of the table.

Adam smiled as his brain registered the striking contrasts between Courtney and her friend. While Suzi was softly rounded, blond and petite—three words usually associated with feminine beauty—he realized that he much preferred Courtney's sleekly sophisticated, tall dark good looks. As a matter of fact, he was crazy about them!

"So, Suzi," Courtney asked, the guarded tone of her voice breaking into Adam's latest revelation, "what brings you all the way down here?"

Adam watched as Suzi's blue eyes, which had been looking so coquettishly into his, clouded with concern. "Oh, Courtney, I was hoping you wouldn't ask me so soon," Suzi whined in a injured-wren voice. "I was hoping we could have a few pleasant moments first. Perhaps even a lovely dinner at a small place I know just outside Somer's Point. It's not a dry town like Ocean City, and we could have had a cocktail or two. My treat!"

"Suzi," Courtney prompted, the honeyed-steel tone of her voice bringing the woman back to attention. "You're as transparent as that very lovely gown you wore to the Authors' Guild banquet last year. You *know* something, don't you? Something I'm not going to like. Spill it."

Lowering her eyes so that Adam couldn't see their expression through the artfully applied black mascara on her long lashes, Suzi replied, "I never could fool you, Courtney, could I? Why, I remember that time at the Oak Room—that's a lovely little club in the Algonquin Hotel," she told Adam as he smiled across the table at her, openly fascinated with the way the woman's tongue seemed to outrun her brain. "They always seem to get just the right act—a brilliant young jazz pianist, a newly discovered soprano whose voice can absolutely reduce you to tears—"

"*Suzi!*"

Suzi slumped against the back of her chair, her cherry-red lower lip pushing forward into a definite pout. "Oh, all right. But remember, you forced it out of me. It's Harry, Courtney. The poor darling. I heard through the grapevine that he's having—how can I say this delicately—financial difficulties."

Adam, who didn't have the time to realize he was picking up on Suzi's talk-first-think-later speech patterns, broke in to the conversation. "How could he? He works for Courtney. His share of her earnings should have him knee deep in clover, even if he didn't have any other clients."

Suzi leaned forward excitedly, nodding her head, speaking to him as if they were the only two people in the room. "That's exactly what I thought, Adam. But the word is that he's been bitten by that nasty little gambling bug. It's embarrassing, truly it is, to watch him scurry around the city, with these very creepy, very large men in dark suits following, yapping at his heels like hungry dogs." She sat back once more, her expression one of eloquent pity. "Poor, *poor* Harry."

Adam suddenly remembered that Courtney was sitting at the head of the table, saying nothing. He also remembered that Sydney was hearing every word.

"Um, Syd?" he prompted. "What do you say you

run over to my condo and get us a couple of pizzas out of the freezer? I think we could all use a snack. Here." He reached into his right pants pocket and withdrew Beatrice's keys, which were unfortunately hooked onto a large brass ring that sported a fluffy pink rabbit's foot. "Take these with you. It's the big green key."

He could see Sydney's reluctance to leave her mother, but the girl rose, coming around the table to take the key ring from Adam's outstretched hand. "*Told* you, Adam," she whispered a bit too loudly as she walked behind him, snapping up the keys. "Mom has *got* to dump him."

Sydney walked through the living room and out the door onto the deck. The silence she left behind her was deafening. Courtney still hadn't spoken, Adam noticed. She hadn't moved a muscle, hadn't given any outward indication of her feelings. She was so in control of her self, so coldly composed, that Adam feared she might just snap in two.

"Courtney?" he asked at last, as Suzi began to squirm in her chair. "Are you all right?"

Her smile froze his question as it left his mouth, so that his words seemed to hang in the air for long seconds, before shattering into a million jagged-edged, dangerous pieces.

"All right, Adam?" she purred finally, rising, her mug in her hand. He felt an almost unconquerable urge to duck, picturing the thing whizzing toward his head. "What a silly question. Why shouldn't I be all right? My good friend Suzi, my daughter, Sydney, and my neighbor, you, were all having such a jolly good time talking about Harry—*my* agent—that I simply didn't want to interrupt your conversation. Would anyone like more coffee? No? Well, I would. Please excuse me while I get myself a refill.''

Suzi's eyes widened, reminding Adam of that deer's startled wide-eyed stare as his headlights had borne down on it late one night on the Atlantic City Expressway. Once Courtney was in the kitchen, standing in front of the counter farthest from the dining room, the woman turned those same frightened eyes to Adam and whispered, ''Oh, Lordy! Do you think it will be painless?''

''Will what be painless?'' he heard himself ask, randomly wondering how many times he was going to let Courtney take him on this roller-coaster ride before he jammed on the brakes. Every time it seemed as if she was going to relax, to open up around him, she jammed the door again, shutting him out. It was funny; he had never thought of himself as a masochist.

''Why, our *deaths,* of course!'' Suzi hissed, spreading her hands. ''Obviously, Adam, you've never seen Courtney in a rage. Well, let me tell you, I have! Just in case you don't know it, Courtney is not always the nice lady we all know and love. Ask anybody. She can be so withdrawn, so collected—so deadly.''

''Deadly?'' Adam repeated, smiling. ''Don't you think you're being a little overdramatic?''

Suzi shook her head so that her blond curls danced around her ears. ''Trust me, Adam. I've personally heard her take one unlucky gossip reporter apart so quietly, with such surgical precision, that it wasn't until the guy tried to move—and came apart like a string of paper dolls—that he'd realized he'd been sliced into ribbons."

Suzi looked so genuinely frightened that Adam had to laugh. "If you knew Courtney would react this way, Suzi," he asked, "why did you come down here to bring her the news? Wouldn't a postcard have been safer? Or maybe a singing telegram?"

"I had to do it. I'm almost the only person in New York who knows where she is. Courtney's my friend, and she's got trouble enough right now—which is why she's here in Ocean City in the first place—without Harry throwing another monkey wrench into her life. I felt I had to tell her what's going on. She'll thank me one day," she ended, shooting a quick look over her shoulder, "if I live that long."

"There is that," Adam agreed, chuckling. "Maybe you'd like to go next door and help Sydney locate those pizzas? It seems to be taking her a long time. The two of you could even go for a walk on the beach, get to know each other better. While you're gone I'll see if I can talk Courtney into a stay of execution."

"Adam, you're a saint! An absolute saint!" Suzi grabbed her cape and flew out the door before Adam realized that, if Courtney was really set on destroying someone, he was now the only target left in sight.

Courtney waited, her back to the dining room, until she heard the door close behind Suzi's departing form. She had heard every word they said. Had they thought she was deaf? *Deadly, am I?* she mused, stirring her coffee and watching the dark whirlpool that formed in the mug, picturing Adam's equally miniaturized body in the center of the mini-maelstrom, going down for the third time. *I'll show them deadly!*

Who did Adam and Suzi think they were, horning in on her life? They didn't know who she was, or where or what she had come from. Who were they to judge her, to intercede for her? She was a big girl; she could take care of herself. Hadn't she been doing it all her life? Who did they think helped her when she was left alone with an infant, no income, no prospects, and a drawer full of bills? Her fairy godmother?

Hardly. *She* had helped herself. She had worked nights as a waitress, with almost half her small salary going to pay the baby-sitters for Sydney. With no high-school diploma behind her, she had studied for her equivalency diploma, hunched over the small kitchen table, rocking Sydney in her infant seat with the toe of one sneakered foot.

Her only respite, her only indulgence, had been the books she had taken by the dozens out of the local free library.

Courtney couldn't even remember how it had begun—the exact moment she had picked up a pencil and a loose-leaf notebook and started to write her own stories. She certainly couldn't remember *why* she had done it. It had simply happened. And the writing had begun to grow, right along with Sydney, who was walking by then and showing her first signs of becoming a real handful.

Three years. Three years of going hungry in order to feed Sydney. Three years of working in greasy all-night diners for minimum wages and scanty tips. Three years of scribbling in notebooks until she convinced herself she could afford a secondhand typewriter. Three years. They had felt like three decades. Three lifetimes.

Harry Gilchrist had taken her away from all that, from the hunger, the grinding poverty, the never-ending fear. Courtney had trusted Harry, so much so that she had allowed her eyes and heart to remain loyally oblivious to his shortcomings long after her mind had opened to the reality of his problems.

Wilbur Langley had told her. Her publisher was a bright man, and he had seen it coming, had seen the changes in Harry and recognized them for what they were. But he had left it up to her to deal with the problem, damn it! Wilbur didn't think it was his place to involve himself in her private life.

Wilbur was her friend, her mentor, and he hadn't interfered.

Suzi was her friend, and Courtney appreciated the concern that had brought her to Ocean City.

Sydney was her daughter, the child of indulgence who couldn't remember the lean years, the child Courtney had left in ignorance of those hard times because she hadn't felt Sydney needed to know about them.

She could forgive Suzi. She understood Sydney. But how did Adam Richardson fit into the picture?

Adam Richardson. Courtney's spine stiffened, and

she realized that she had been standing at the counter so long that the small of her back had begun to ache. If she wanted to kill anybody, it was Adam Richardson. If she thought her life had been a mess for the past six months—dealing with her writer's block and her growing problems with Harry—that now seemed like a walk in the park compared to what she had been through since she'd met Adam Richardson.

The man was a menace. He disturbed her peace. He was a moneyed vagabond who had never known what it was like to go to bed hungry. He had charmed her impressionable daughter into giving out family secrets like Halloween treats. He was too damned nosy.

He makes me cry, she told herself, squeezing her eyes shut. *He makes me feel. He makes me want. He makes me need.*

"Courtney?"

At the sound of Adam's voice, coming so close to her ear, Courtney whirled around so quickly that she nearly collided with his leanly muscled chest. She felt his hands come out to grab her upper arms, steadying her while at the same time sending a convulsive shiver of longing through her body. "Are you all right?"

It would be so easy; so easy to collapse against his strength again; so easy to let her guard down once more and let him take her back to the woman she had been last night in his arms. No one would describe that woman as cold, or deadly.

She had been more alive, more tinglingly aware of herself as a woman in those few glorious minutes than she had been since she had come to Rob all those years ago on their wedding night and learned what it meant to be loved.

Courtney gave her head a quick shake, deliberately bringing herself back to reality. "I'm fine, Adam," she said, pulling away from him. "Did you think I was going to burst into hysterics in front of you all? Suzi meant well, but she didn't tell me anything I didn't already know."

She looked up into Adam's compassionate gray eyes as he asked quietly, "It isn't just the gambling. He's been skimming, too, hasn't he, Courtney? Placing bets with your money?"

I'll give him one thing—he sure knows where to aim his darts, Courtney thought, feeling her hackles beginning to rise in spite of herself. "Congratulations, Mr. Richardson!" she exclaimed brightly. "And for that correct answer you have won the grand prize—an all-expenses-paid, fun-filled week on the beautiful, the exotic, the magnificent—moon!"

Adam winced, his expression a parody of fear. "Wow! Suzi said you could be tough. The moon, huh? I just hope you let me pack my woollies first, because it's eight to five you'll make sure I land on the dark side." His expression sobered. "But Harry *has* been gambling with your money, hasn't he?"

Suzi would have been flabbergasted if she could have seen the ease with which Adam turned Courtney's famous ice-maiden image into a soggy mass of half-set gelatin. Even his latest rather weak attempt at humor and stubborn tenacity appealed to her. *Everything* about Adam Richardson appealed to her, damn

him. Courtney laughed, the sound hollow, as she
walked past him to sit in a chair in the living room.
Most of it was out in the open now. She might as well
let him have the rest of it.

"Of course he has," she admitted on a sigh. "I
discovered it for the first time almost two years ago,
but Harry paid back every cent and then promised
me—on his knees—that he'd never do it again."

She closed her eyes, suddenly very weary. Just how
many hours of sleep had she had in the last twenty-
four? Two? Three? "Harry believed in me when nobody else did. What other choice did I have? I had to
believe him."

"And you have an accountant, right?" Adam asked,
slipping into the couch that sat at a right angle to
Courtney's chair. "Didn't he pick up on it, too?"

Her weariness disappeared. This had gone on long
enough, Courtney decided—too long. She had stood
in the kitchen, hating him, and now she was telling
him things she hadn't even told Wilbur. She had
planned to rip a verbal strip off Adam's inquisitive
hide and show him the door. What had happened to
that plan? Why was she sitting here, spilling her guts
like some suspect being grilled by the police?

"No. You see, I finished high school with corre-
spondence courses, and math was never my best subject," she heard herself explain. "Harry always acted
as my accountant. From the very beginning, the money
had been good—so much more than I had ever seen
in my life—and I saw no reason to make any changes.
After a few years, Harry even gave up the rest of his

clients to become my personal manager, press agent, traveling companion on book tours—everything. He became the father I never had. I *trusted* him."

Adam nodded, seemingly accepting her explanation, no hint of condescension or pity on his handsome face at her admission that she had not graduated from high school in the usual way. "So how did you finally figure it out?"

Courtney spread her hands and then clenched them tight. Her hands fluttered once more, then settled in her lap. "I don't know. It wasn't one thing—it was a lot of things, a lot of little things. After the first time around it was easier to spot the problems the second time."

"But it's even worse now, isn't it? Harry is doing flips because of your writer's block. He gets a chunk of money when this book is completed, right?"

Courtney nodded. "For an idle-rich beach bum, Adam Richardson, you think pretty good," she quipped, trying a weak smile and finding that it didn't hurt—much. "Harry's over his ears in debt, and this time I've refused to bail him out. We had a flaming fight the other night on the phone, as Sydney has, I assume, already told you." She lowered her head, knowing she couldn't look into Adam's eyes or else chance dissolving into stupid self-pitying tears. Courtney was getting very weary of tears.

"So, what are you going to do?"

"I've fired him," she whispered, her voice breaking as tears stung at the back of her eyes. "He was my friend, the only real friend I've ever had—except for

Rob. Do you know what it's like to be betrayed by a friend? Even so, firing Harry was the most difficult, heartrending thing I've ever had to do.''

"'A friend should bear his friend's infirmities, / But Brutus makes mine greater than they are.'''

Courtney's head snapped up and she looked at Adam. "With Harry in the role of Brutus? That certainly hits it right on the head, doesn't it? Good old Shakespeare. He had a saying to fit every situation, every mood. Thanks, Adam.''

"It just seemed appropriate.'' Adam grinned at her, and for some reason Courtney knew she was going to be all right. She was going to make it. The worst was over.

She leaned forward, suddenly wanting him to know everything now. "I'm going to continue paying him a salary—sort of a pension. Harry will be all right—if he can give up his love for the ponies, that is, and nobody breaks his knees. He's a good man, Adam. He's just weak.''

"I know,'' Adam said, reaching to take her hand. "He's also in a very expensive institution in upstate New York learning how to beat his addiction, courtesy of Courtney Blackmun.''

It was a good thing she was sitting down, for Adam's last words would have knocked her off her feet. "How—how could you know that? He just got there last night. *Nobody* knows that.''

She watched as a very becoming flush reddened Adam's deep tan. "Beatrice told me. I asked her to check your Harry out after Sydney told me he was giving you trouble. What I didn't know was the manner of his addiction. I guess I just assumed it was drugs. Suzi helped with the rest.''

Come on, Courtney, her mind screamed inside her pounding head, *get mad. Get really mad. Who does this bozo think he is, using his high-level associations to take a voyeuristic peek into your private life? Is this how he gets his kicks?*

"You did *what*?'' was all Courtney could ask. She croaked the words actually, for she was still having trouble assimilating the scope of what Adam had done. "Why?"

Adam squeezed her hand. "He came down hard on Sydney,'' he told her, the smoothly cut planes of his face going rigid. "He upset you. Be happy all I did was check up on him. My first thought was to look him up and rearrange his face.''

Courtney fell back against the chair. "He came down hard on Sydney? *My* Sydney—the twentieth century's answer to Joshua, who is capable of single-handedly bringing down whole school systems with a single toot?'' she said incredulously, barely keeping back the laughter bubbling in her throat. "I left her with him for one weekend and he nearly had to check into a rest home to recuperate. She was a holy terror! Tell me, Adam, did Beatrice tell you how old Harry is?''

Adam shook his head. "Forty-five? Fifty?''

"Seventy-four,'' Courtney answered, giggling. "He *had* to ground her, before she hot-wired his pacemaker! Good Lord, don't tell me you really fell for

Sydney's ridiculousness? Why, Syd has called him Uncle Harry since she learned to talk. We even lived with him for a while—although I doubt Sydney remembers it—until my first book came out." Her emerald eyes narrowed. "What else did she say about Harry?"

"Just that you should dump him," Adam admitted, looking sheepish, as if he had finally figured out that Sydney had been leading him down the garden path with one of her stories. "I have a lot to learn about thirteen-year-old girls, don't I?"

Courtney chuckled. "Volumes! But you know, I admit that Sydney has been right to worry about the relationship between Harry and me. It wasn't as if she would've had to be a rocket scientist to figure out that our relations have been strained for the past two years. I probably should have been more open with her, explaining the situation. But the child certainly took literary license with the parts of the story she didn't know. Let that be a lesson to you, Adam. Never believe a woman when she's trying to get something from you."

Adam's winglike brows, the brows that so intrigued her, met together over his long eyes. "And what, pray tell, was Sydney trying to get from me?"

Courtney shrugged, knowing she had gone too far. What did Sydney want from Adam? What did Sydney want from any eligible man she met? She wanted what Courtney thought she'd found in Harry—a father. "I don't know," she lied quickly, "but, if I were you, I'd be very careful."

Adam rose to stand in front of her chair, his hands on the overstuffed arms, effectively pinning her to the seat. "And what does her mother want from me, do you think?" His voice was low, seductive and very, very unnerving. "I'm getting mixed signals from her right now, and I'm terribly confused. What do you think I should do?"

Courtney couldn't help herself. She was back under Adam's spell, willing or unwilling, and she couldn't think about anything other than the prospect of his mouth on hers, the heady sensation she had found in his arms, the comfortable calm she had felt lying close beside his warm strong body.

She watched, fascinated, as his head dipped toward hers. Her eyes slowly closed as she anticipated the lightning bolt of sensation that she knew would soon be cutting a hot pulsing path through her body.

He was everything she despised—aimless, a playboy who lived through and for his personal pleasures.

He was everything she admired—caring, compassionate, a man who had reminded her that not all of life had to be a struggle.

She could feel his breath, warm and caressing against her cheek, and her anticipation grew. But then without warning he was gone, and it was as if all the sunlight had gone out of her life with him.

"Methinks I hear the gentle footfalls of Sydney and the book reviewer from hell on the steps outside," he informed her, falling back onto the couch. "We'll pick this up later, if I don't have another sudden attack of sanity."

"Sanity, Adam?" Courtney asked, straightening in her chair. "So you agree that what the two of us were about to do—with my child apt to come barreling in here at any moment—is some form of insanity?"

Adam grinned, and Courtney felt another crack open in the thirteen-year layer of ice around her heart. "Yeah," he crooned, rolling his eyes, "but what a way to go!"

They were both laughing as a wind-tousled Sydney burst through the door into the living room, with Suzi, her smooth cheeks flushed from the wind, her blue eyes sparkling like sun on the ocean, close on her heels. They looked like naughty children who had a secret between them—a secret too wonderful, too delicious, to keep to themselves.

Obviously her daughter agreed. "Mom!" Sydney shouted, running up behind the chair to throw her arms around a startled Courtney. "You'll never believe it. It's, like, totally rad! Suzi has invited me to go back to New York with her, to enroll in the private day school she went to when she was a kid."

"But, Syd," Courtney interrupted, instantly recognizing that her daughter's departure would leave her alone in Ocean City with Adam. "You just got here."

"But, Mom," Sydney countered with the sort of maddening logic that Courtney had long ago become accustomed to hearing from her daughter, "I'm thirteen. I belong in school. And get this—they don't require uniforms! I can stay with Suzi, too, until you finish the book and come home. She has this darling old housekeeper, Mrs. O'Reilly, who makes the best chocolate-chip cookies in the universe. Suzi's got a condo that overlooks the park! Can you believe it? I can go back to New York! Isn't that great? Isn't that just totally awesome?''

Courtney, her breathing constricted by Sydney's convulsive grip on her neck, swiveled her eyes to the right so that she could look at Adam. He was sitting very still on the couch. ''Totally awesome, Syd,'' he said, smiling broadly.

But he was looking at Courtney.

Chapter Seven

Panic!

That was the only word for it.

Complete, total, absolute panic.

"Or gross stupidity," Courtney muttered, allowing the vertical blinds to slide back into place as she turned her back on the view of sunlit beach and rolling surf.

How had she gotten herself into this situation? What strange madness, what temporary aberration, had allowed her to talk herself into letting Sydney go tripping back to New York City with Suzi Harper?

"Why such a halfway measure? As long as I was doing it, why didn't I just pack Syd off to Disney World with Moe, Larry and Curly? They would have had a ball," she groused, flopping onto a chair in the suddenly empty condo, knowing she was being unfair. Suzi Harper wasn't incompetent. Far from it. Just the fact that Suzi had hit Courtney below the belt—helpfully pointing out how much happier Sydney would be once she was back in school, which was, by the by, where the child *belonged*—was proof positive of her friend's intelligence.

It was just that everything had happened so quickly, catching Courtney totally off guard. One minute Sydney was there and the next she was going blithely out the front door, laughing and throwing kisses to her deserted mother.

"Kids ought to come with warning labels," Courtney decided, her chin resting on her chest. "Like cigarettes. Caution. Raising children may be hazardous to your emotional health." So saying, she leaned forward and picked up her cigarette case, taking refuge in her most dangerous vice. "My most dangerous vice—except for Adam," she concluded, exhaling a thin stream of smoke as she addressed the glowing tip of the cigarette. "Adam Richardson. Let me tell you, buster, now we're talking *vice!*"

What was bothering her so much? Was it the way Adam had immediately taken Sydney's side when the child had pleaded with Courtney to let her return to New York? Was it the way all his arguments—added to those of Sydney and Suzi—had made so much sense?

Was it the fact that he had so effortlessly taken charge? He'd treated them all to a quick bite to eat and then had packed Sydney's suitcases into the trunk of Suzi's car and waved them on their way. Everything had happened almost before Courtney had had a chance to catch her breath.

Courtney crushed the half-smoked cigarette in the ashtray, disgusted with herself. It was none of that. She was alone now; it was time to face facts. The answer was simply another question: why hadn't she gone back to New York, as well?

Nothing was holding her in Ocean City. The problem of Harry was, at long last, on its way to being solved. She had, thanks either to coming to grips with Harry's problem or the cleansing storm of tears she'd had in Adam's arms, finally broken through her first writer's block.

There was absolutely no reason for Courtney Blackmun, supposed adult in charge of her own destiny, to remain in Ocean City. Not a single solitary reason.

Save one.

Adam Richardson.

Adam Richardson, with his irresistible charm, his arm comfortingly wrapping around her waist as she had stepped back from the car after kissing Sydney goodbye.

Adam Richardson, with the "Wanna play house?" waggle of his infuriatingly adorable eyebrows as Suzi's lemon-yellow BMW backed out of the driveway.

Adam Richardson, the man who knew full well that the only reason she was remaining behind Ocean City could be summed up in those same two words: Adam Richardson.

"Damn the man!" Courtney exploded. She stood and began pacing the honey-beige living-room carpet, hoping to burn up some of the nervous energy that was rapidly turning her into a basket case.

She should go downstairs to her makeshift office and work. Elliot was waiting for her. She'd left the poor guy standing at the side of a San Francisco ballroom, his lean muscular frame languidly supporting a pillar as he stared through the dancers floating across the floor in a graceful waltz. He was bored, Elliot was, waiting for the heroine to appear and throw a monkey wrench into his well-ordered life. It was never polite to keep a hero waiting.

Courtney headed for the circular staircase, then stopped. Let him wait. Elliot was controllable—he'd do what she wanted when she wanted. Courtney smiled evilly. That was one of the perks of writing. She had total control over her characters. They talked when she wanted them to, said what she wanted them to say and faded to black whenever she pressed the right button.

If only she could say the same about Adam. Try as she might, whether waking or sleeping, she couldn't seem to get Adam to fade to black. He was always there, in her mind, in her heart, in full living color, eating away at thirteen years of purpose.

Yes, that was it. That was what was bothering her. *Purpose.* Courtney was all purpose; her every move, her every thought, had always been directed toward goals she had set for herself. And when she had reached those goals she had established new ones.

As Adam had admitted to her when they first met, he had no purpose, no goals in life, no real function—

unless it was to drive her crazy. He was a wealthy aimless wastrel, obviously content to be what he was, perhaps even proud of his uselessness.

If he had no potential, no talent, it would't bother her so much. But Adam was an extremely intelligent man. "He even quotes Shakespeare, for crying out loud," Courtney exploded, storming into the kitchen to make herself a cup of instant coffee.

But the worst, the very worst thing about Adam was that he was getting to her, softening her, even clouding her judgment to the point that she was doubting the tenets she had lived by for thirteen long years. He was undermining her sense of purpose, contaminating her with his smile, his easy ways, his gentle mind-destroying loving.

Courtney had made a decision. She abandoned the cup of coffee and raced down the steps to her bedroom. She had to get out of here—now, while there was still time. She had to get away before she saw him again, before he smiled at her again, before he touched her again.

She threw her suitcase onto the bed and began flinging random bits of clothing into it as she sped around the room, opening drawers and tossing bras, sweatshirts and nighties over her shoulder.

Panic. The word was close, but it wasn't right.

The correct word was *self-preservation.*

She could have gone.

The thought kept Adam smiling as he speed-read his way through the thick packet of documents Beatrice had sent by courier from his office in Trenton. He scribbled notes in the margins, intelligible only to himself and his assistant, circled questionable passages, then stuffed the papers into the return envelope Beatrice had provided and phoned for a delivery service to pick up the packet in the morning.

The same thought had him humming as he stood beneath the needle-sharp sting of the shower two hours later. *She could have gone. She could have gone.*

"But she didn't," he said as he grinned into the small circle he had cleared on the steam-clouded mirror over the sink, laughing out loud as his shaving-cream-slathered face leered back at him. "She stayed."

That meant something. It *had* to mean something. Courtney Blackmun wasn't the sort of person to allow her life to be ruled by a whim; nor was she the free and easy kind of female who would ever indulge in a mindless romantic fling with any available man. She had known what she was doing when she let Sydney leave, even if he was going to have to be the person to tell her why she had done it.

Whether she was willing to admit it or not, he and Courtney had made some sort of commitment to each other that night in front of the fireplace, the night she had allowed him to kiss her, comfort her and hold her close. That commitment—and *attraction*—was keeping Courtney here in Ocean City.

Lord, how he was attracted to her. Intellectually, as well as physically. He couldn't believe it was possible to remain heart-whole for thirty-five years only to have his entire world turned upside down in the space of a few hours by a green-eyed, sharp-tongued, damnably independent female who was fighting her attraction to him every inch of the way.

He admired everything about Courtney—her looks, her passion, her love for her child, her loyalty to an old friend, her clear-eyed, sometimes rigidly inflexible way of looking at the world. Yes, he even admired her failings. She hadn't had it easy, Adam already knew that from the scant scraps of information Courtney had revealed to him, but she had come away from her bad experiences a survivor, a total woman and a complete lady.

Her success as a writer was her magna-cum-laude degree from the college of hard knocks, and she had every right to be proud of herself.

She was honest rather than cynical, hardworking rather than whining, giving rather than grasping. She was a fighter—and she didn't have a selfish bone in her lovely lovable body.

Her only real blind spot, as far as Adam could see, was her determination to cushion her child from her own past, from the reality that life wasn't always easy or even fair. Sydney was definitely a child of privilege, and Courtney would, he was sure, gladly die rather than have the child experience any of the privations of her own childhood. How could he blame her for loving her child that much?

Standing in front of the open closet, randomly selecting his clothes for the evening, Adam remembered something else about Courtney. She thought he was one of the idle rich, a man content to live off the fat of another man's hard work, which was the impression he had given when they had met.

He also remembered that he had been about to correct her wrong impression when Suzi Harper had shown up on Courtney's doorstep, so that Courtney still didn't know the truth about him.

"Yet she still stayed," Adam told himself, his left eyebrow flying high as he considered what to do next. "It's too late for the truth now, even if I wanted to tell her. Besides, this is what I wanted. I had to know if I was still real or if I've been turned into a salable product.

"Yes, Courtney's got to trust me because I'm me, be attracted to me because I'm me—maybe even fall in *love* with me, damn it!" he growled as he shut the closet door with enough force to rattle the china shepherdess figurine on a nearby table. "If she hated the thought that inherited money paved my way in life, I can't take the chance she'll think I expect *what* I really am to take precedence over *who* I am by telling her the truth now. No. She's got to want Adam Richardson, the *man,* just as I want Courtney Blackmun, the *woman.* It's the only way."

As he climbed into a pair of loden green slacks and sat on the edge of the bed to slip on socks and shoes, he found himself thinking back to his days as a running back at Princeton, humoring himself by comparing his romantic strategy to offensive football. He likened the events of the past few days to the broken-field running he had done in college, having to fight his way past Courtney's initial resistance for every inch of progress.

Sydney's sudden appearance as an unexpected tackler just as he had thought he was gaining ground had come from nowhere to hit him from his blind side, throwing him for a loss. Sydney had made him adjust his game plan, that was for sure. After completing one pass for a first down, he had been forced back to grinding out short gains—playing the waiting game.

Who could have thought his most effective blocker would have been a petite somewhat scatterbrained blond book reviewer, and that in one blinding flash he would see a wedge of daylight open in front of him, a clear path that could lead him to victory?

"The field's wide open now," he told himself as he pushed his head through the opening of a butter-yellow turtleneck. He ran a comb through his hair, examined his reflection in the bedroom mirror and almost as an afterthought splashed some cologne on his lean cheeks before heading for the door.

His muscles were taut, his heart was pounding, reminding him how he had felt during his college playing days when he had broken away from the last tackler to see that nothing but green grass and yard markers lay between him and the goalposts.

As he stood in the early darkness on the deck outside Courtney's condo, his hand poised to knock, he couldn't resist whispering, "It's *touchdown* time!"

She had almost made it.

Courtney's bags were packed and stacked in the hall

outside her bedroom door.

She had located the switches controlling the heat and turned them down to the maintenance level.

She had thrown the rest of the fresh meat into the freezer and poured the contents of an opened carton of milk down the sink, knowing it would only turn sour if she were to leave it in the refrigerator.

She had unplugged the toaster, the microwave and the coffee maker.

She had even stripped the beds she and Sydney had slept in, washed and dried the sheets, then cleaned the bathrooms, her years of efficient housekeeping making it impossible for her to leave the condo any less orderly than she had found it. At least that was what Courtney had told herself as she knelt on the tile floor, scouring the pink bathtub.

She had totally depleted her store of lame excuses, exhausted her supply of delaying tactics, run out of unconscious maneuvers that would keep her there until Adam—the big bad wolf—came huffing and puffing at her door once more.

Yes, she had almost made it. She had almost been able to walk away, or slink away, as she had termed it to herself. It was dark outside—after six o'clock. Suppertime. She had no more reasons to delay her departure.

Wait a minute. She *had* made it. She *was* ready to go. She was ready to throw her suitcases into the trunk of the Mercedes, slide her tail between her legs, and slink out of town. All that remained was to *do* it.

So why wasn't she doing it?

"Where the hell is he?" Courtney's words, spoken so vehemently in the quiet condo, slammed against the walls to come careening back at her, laughing at her futile struggle to break herself free from the inevitable.

Courtney sat down in a living-room chair, a single small light burning over the kitchen sink the only illumination in the otherwise dark condo, and waited.

Courtney faced the truth at last. She wasn't going anywhere.

He used his special knock. She had heard it only a half dozen times before, but she recognized it as a part of him. She waited until he knocked again, then rose, her mind on automatic pilot, her body throbbing with life, and walked to the door.

"I froze the meat and poured all the milk down the sink," she said dully as she opened the door and stood back to let him enter. "And the heat is turned back to the maintenance level."

She watched, fascinated, as Adam's expressive gray eyes registered a quick confusion, followed just as swiftly by understanding. It was amazing, but she was sure he knew exactly what had gone on during his absence, that he knew she had nearly run away. Even more amazing was her certainty that he wasn't angry or even hurt. He seemed to simply accept it, the same way he accepted the fact she was still here.

She watched dumbly as he walked across the room to pick up her coat, which had been lying across the back of a chair. "I was in the mood to go out to eat anyway," she heard Adam say as he arranged the coat around her shoulders, his fingertips trailing lightly along her throat before moving away. "As far as the heat goes, I'll see what I can do about that later."

"Oh, is that right?" Courtney responded, leaning back against him, giving in to the shiver of anticipation that tickled her spine. She turned her head and lifted her gaze to his laughing gray eyes, her mind and body at last totally in tune with one another, and realized that all her preparations for flight had only been delaying tactics meant to keep her from thinking, meant to keep her here—with Adam.

"You were so!"

"I was not!" Adam neatly slid the long spatula beneath the two fried eggs and deftly flipped them over, the yolks remaining intact. "Ah! Another Richardson masterpiece. Quick, woman, hand me that plate. You said you like your eggs over easy."

Courtney—dressed only in a pair of Adam's running shorts and one of his long-sleeved white shirts, its collar turned up à-la-Hepburn, her long black hair tumbling around her shoulders—slipped from the counter to hold out her empty plate.

"They look delicious," she said as he turned the sizzling eggs onto the plate. Giving in to impulse, she went up on tiptoe to kiss his cheek. "My compliments to the chef," she offered, walking toward the dining room. "And you were so!" she called over her shoulder, continuing their friendly argument.

Adam added a little more butter to the frying pan

before pouring his own whipped eggs into it and stirring them with a fork. He liked his eggs scrambled, rather the way his brain had felt these past few days. "You've got to be kidding, Court. Drooling over Suzi Harper? Me? That woman's got a mind like those sample houses builders put up for prospective buyers—lovely to look at, but when you open the door there's nobody home. Eat your eggs before they get cold. I'll just be a minute. And save me a piece of toast."

Courtney looked around Beatrice's dining room, the decor more to her liking each time she saw it. After enjoying a candlelight dinner at a nearby inn, Adam had suggested they adjourn to his condo—the one that still had heat. They had sat in front of the roaring fireplace and talked, and kissed, and talked and kissed some more, Adam holding her close to his side until Courtney had fallen asleep on the couch.

She couldn't remember the last time she had felt so safe, so unthreatened, yet so inspired and, yes, even aroused. But Adam, bless him, had been a gentleman, just as he had that first night in front of the fire.

She smiled as she bit into a piece of toast. Waking in Beatrice's French Provincial living room early this morning had shocked her for a moment. But a few minutes later, after Adam had climbed the circular staircase carrying the shirt and shorts and tossed them at her nonchalantly, saying only, "I've already laid out towels for your shower," she had soon relaxed and begun to enjoy herself. It was rather like being at camp, she had decided, even though she had never been at camp—or believed that there was such a thing as a coed camp.

Looking up at Adam, dressed in jeans and a black sweater, his dark hair still damp and adorably tousled, as he slid into the chair across from her, a plate of steaming scrambled eggs in his hand, Courtney felt a slight embarrassed flush coloring her cheeks. He was so good to look at. Even with his morning beard shadowing his face, he was the most handsome desirable man she had ever seen.

She could still feel the tender roughness of Adam's hands as they had held her last night, molding her softness to fit so perfectly against his lean muscular form. She could still taste the intoxicating flavor of his kisses....

"Suzi Harper is not stupid, Adam," she blurted hastily, knowing her thoughts could lead her into trouble. "She's a damn good book reviewer—incisive, unbiased, well-grounded in her field. She's sharp as a tack."

Adam raised his eyebrows, clearly not believing a word she had said. "Right. And I'm really Peter O'Toole. You always knew my English accent was a phony, didn't you? I was really born in New Jersey—in Bayonne."

Courtney shook her head, smiling at his wit. "No, seriously, Adam, Suzi is a smart cookie. Oh, I admit that she comes off looking slightly scatterbrained—"

"But she was right about Sydney," Adam said, raising his hands as if in surrender. "I think the two of them are going to be just fine. To tell you the truth,

Court, it's New York I'm worried about. The Big Apple may never be the same after those two get through with it.''

Courtney laughed aloud, before taking one last bite of egg. It really was very good. Adam was a good cook, but then, it seemed he was good at a lot of things. Making her laugh was only one of them. ''Let me tell you something, my fine egg-frying friend,'' she countered, waving a piece of toast at him. ''Sydney was *born* for New York. She's made a real project of it. I think she knows every museum, statue, playhouse and subway station in Manhattan.''

Adam, also finished eating, pushed his plate away and picked up his half-empty mug of coffee. ''Did you say subway station? You mean you actually let her ride the subways?''

Courtney stood, picking up both their plates. Was she wrong, or was that fatherly concern she heard in Adam's voice? ''Only between the hours of nine and five, Adam, and *never* alone.''

''Because otherwise you'd murder her?''

''Ex-ac-a-tickly,'' Courtney purred, whisking past him to the kitchen. ''I've found that the best way to mother Sydney is with a long leash. That way she doesn't tug on it so often.''

As she neared the sink Adam came up behind her, slipping his hands around her waist. ''I love it when you're motherly,'' he growled, nuzzling her neck.

She almost dropped the plates. What was it about this man that had her turning into a formless mound of jelly each time he touched her? "Adam," she half-ordered, half-pleaded, "you have to let me go."

"Not until you say you're sorry," he responded irrepressibly, his fingers busily unbuttoning the top button of her shirt.

Courtney could barely hear her own voice over the wild pounding of her heart. "So-sorry for what? You've lost me." Was this the same comfortable Adam who hadn't pressed her for anything more than kisses last night? The same understanding Adam who had seemed so willing to play the game according to her unspoken rules?

"Sorry for saying that I was drooling over Suzi Harper."

"Y-you're back to that?" Adam's hands were moving now, stroking, caressing, teasing, provoking. Courtney bent her knees slightly, lowering the plates to the countertop, then allowed her head to lean back against his broad chest.

As his hands molded and cupped her breasts, he began nibbling at her earlobe, his warm breath sending an expectant shiver down her spine. Courtney had allowed him this liberty twice before—allowed herself this pleasure twice before—and he hadn't demanded anything more. She decided to play his game for a while, just to see what would happen next. "And what happens to me if I refuse to apologize?"

He spoke softly, and in a very bad imitation of every old war movie she had ever seen. "So, Madam Blackmun. You choose to remain silent. Zere will be conse-quences. Ve haff *vays* off making you talk."

Two could play this game. She could sense her bare feet moving, almost as if they were following an unspoken command, as she slowly turned in his arms, then began running her hands beneath the hem of his sweater, the muscles of his bared skin rippling beneath her fingertips. Standing on tiptoe, she felt her lips soften as they made contact with the masculine stubble on the sharp angle of his chin.

"You haff vays?" Courtney raised her head to gaze wonderingly into Adam's eyes. He was looking down at her as if she were the most beautiful, the most desirable creature in the world. In the universe.

It was strange, but his lovemaking seemed even more intense in the daylight than it had in the warm glow from the fire. Her reaction to him frightened her even as she gloried in the feeling of his hands against her bared flesh. She swallowed, hard, and took a single backward step—the hardest step she had ever taken—drawing the shirt closed with trembling fingers.

It was time for sanity. The time for games was over. It was important to get back to the real world, before she took a step she wasn't ready to take, hadn't planned to take. "I—I have to leave now, Adam," she whispered shakily. "I've got to get to work. I—I'm sorry."

Adam's hands fell to his sides and he smiled, just as if the short, potentially dangerous assault on her senses had never taken place. "Time for the diligent worker to get back to her grindstone, huh? I guess I'll be walking the beach alone this morning."

"Some of us have to work, Adam," she said, her own ardor cooling as his words made her remember the vast difference between them. He probably hadn't worked a day in his life.

"Not this someone," he answered airily. "Although I may break down and do these dishes. But you go ahead, Court. I'll come by later to rescue you from your computer. I took your extra key last night, remember?"

"That's it?" she asked, staring at him. Surely he wouldn't give up so easily. He wasn't going to try to talk her into walking the beach with him? He wasn't going to throw out any hints that they should drive down to Cape May for the day?

"That's it, Court," he said, turning toward the sink, turning his back on her confusion. "Don't ask me to work and I won't stop you from working. To each his own, right? Don't work too hard. See you later."

And that *had* been it, Courtney thought as she crossed the sand to mount the steps to her condo. He hadn't argued with her. He had simply stood back and watched her walk out of the kitchen, out of the condo. He was back to being the undemanding Adam she had begun to trust.

Courtney didn't know whether she wanted to thank him or slug him!

Elliot wanted to hit her—or kiss her. She was the most exasperating female he'd ever had the misfortune to encounter, and he'd met his share of women. Women wanted him, which was fortunate, for Elliot enjoyed women. But this one was different. This one was fighting him at every turn, even though he was sure she wasn't immune to him.

Heaven help him, he wasn't immune to her.

Courtney sat back to read what she had written. Elliot was in up to his knees now, whether he knew it or not. Her reluctant hero—one time gunslinger, sometimes gambler, full-time womanizer—had met his match. She lit a cigarette, then just as quickly put it out. Adam would be coming over any minute and he'd be able to smell it on her breath. For reasons she refused to investigate, that idea distressed her.

A shadow fell over the computer screen as Adam leaned down to read over her shoulder, just as if the thought of him had conjured him up in person. "Who's Elliot? Your hero? What kind of hero is named Elliot? Shouldn't it be Jonas, or Hawk, or Jason?"

"Or Adam?" Courtney allowed him to rub her back, his hands easing the tension she hadn't realized had been tightening the muscles between her shoulder blades. She hadn't heard him come into the room, which showed her how involved she had been with her book. She looked at the clock face displayed on the computer screen. Had she really been working for six hours?

"Or Adam. What's wrong with Adam? It's a good name—solid, dependable. Of course, there was that little problem in Eden, but that was all Eve's fault, anyway."

Courtney wrinkled her nose as she looked up at him. "My hero, blaming a woman for his own downfall. How terribly heroic. I think I'll stick with Elliot, thanks just the same."

"To each his own, I guess," he answered, leaning

down to kiss the nape of her neck. "You about ready for a break? The sun will be going down soon and I thought we could take a quick walk on the beach before dinner."

Courtney shot out of her chair. "Dinner! Oh, my God, I totally forgot about dinner. I froze everything yesterday, and I wanted to cook for you tonight. Do you have anything in your— No, never mind. I'll defrost something. I have the microwave." She leaned down to move the mouse and hit the Quit button.

"I do this all the time," she said, almost to herself. "I get so wrapped up in things, so damn carried away, that I forget everything else. There," she said, ejecting the disks and switching off the machine, "all done and saved for posterity." She turned from the computer, nearly barrelling into Adam in her haste to get upstairs to the kitchen.

"Whoa!" he warned, steadying her. "Do you always turn into a quivering wreck when you do something human, like forgetting about dinner? Relax. We won't starve. We can go out for dinner again tonight."

Courtney bristled, pulling away from him. She didn't know why she was becoming angry; she just was. "What do you mean—when I do something *human*? Are you implying that I think I'm *super*human?"

Adam shrugged. "I don't know, Court. You tell me. We were up half the night talking—not that I'm complaining—and up just as early this morning. While I took a nap this afternoon, you were over here working away on your latest epic. Can't you ever relax? Forget about the book for a while. It's not going anywhere without you."

She couldn't stop herself. She wanted to, but she couldn't do it. She felt all her nerves tautening, as if a giant spring was being overwound inside her head.

Courtney felt the tension between her shoulder blades coming back at double the force. "Precisely! The book goes nowhere without me. My career goes nowhere without me. My future goes nowhere without me. For a lot of years, Chester, while you were blithely clipping coupons from your daddy's bonds, I was clipping cents-off coupons to buy groceries. Relaxing is just fine—if you can afford it. *I* can't."

"Chester," Adam repeated, shaking his head. "I take it this is not a friendly argument—not that I think we're arguing, you understand. It was only a comment, not a judgment. You're taking this too seriously. I didn't mean any harm. Look, Court—"

"No—*you* look! Wilbur may call it my throwback to a Great Depression era mentality, and I might know deep down inside that I'll never have to go back where I was fourteen years ago, but there are some things about me that you have no right to poke your aristocratic nose into—and yes, I know my grammar is going all to hell. I'm angry, and when I'm angry I end my sentences with prepositions. So sue me. Tell me you never want to see me again. I don't care what you do. Only don't think that just because you caught me when I was down and I've stupidly talked to you about my problems, I've given you carte blanche to crawl inside my mind, okay!"

Chapter Eight

Adam took one step back, amazed, as Courtney flashed past him, a vibrant blur of soft violet scent, flying black hair and coral sweatsuit, obviously intent on putting as much space between the two of them as the condo allowed.

How stupid could he be? Talk about pushing the wrong button! There were times Adam wished Courtney had come into his life equipped with an instruction booklet, so that he would be able to refer to it for directions, and warnings.

Not that he would have been attracted to an uncomplicated woman, or a woman like so many he had known, who depended on a flashy outward show to hide their real selves. Oh, yes, Courtney could wear a professional facade, but only for protection, never for illusion. Adam knew that Courtney was—long after the need had ceased to exist—still compelled to prove herself, over and over again.

Adam might know about her past, but he also could guiltily acknowledge that he was a long way from understanding it. He had been born into a loving family complete with the proverbial silver spoon in his mouth, so he had no similar experiences to draw on, no parallels to use for comparison. Trying for a bit of humor, teasing her for what he saw as an endearing trait, he had unwittingly steered into the floating mine field of her past, and it had blown up in his face.

He heard cabinet doors opening and slamming in the kitchen above him. At least it appeared that she was still planning to feed him. "Arsenic on toast points, probably," he mused aloud, "not that I don't deserve it. Tell me, Richardson, how did you ever get so far in this world, suffering as you do from terminal foot-in-mouth disease?"

He climbed the wrought-iron circular staircase, his steps dragging slightly as he racked his brain for a way to smooth the waters his thoughtless remarks had ruffled, already knowing that his famous charm wasn't going to get him out of this one. He had blundered—badly.

He stood just outside the kitchen, watching Courtney as she raced from one end of the counter to the other like a woman possessed, throwing a hunk of frozen ground beef into the microwave, then tearing open a bag of frozen French fries and arranging them on a cookie sheet.

A can of corn, creamed, the way he liked it best,

stood next to the can opener. Bending to reach into the cabinet under the sink, she dug a large Bermuda onion out of a plastic basket and slammed the unlucky vegetable onto a cutting board.

Just as she was about to pick up a rather nasty-looking knife, Adam stepped onto the tile, his footfalls purposely heavy, to alert her to his presence. "Don't take it out on the onion, Court. It doesn't deserve it. Besides, I'm a bigger target."

She remained still, frozen like the meat in the microwave, yet he thought he could detect some slight thawing around her brittle edges. He moved closer, daring to lay a hand on her shoulder. "Courtney, sweetheart," he said sincerely, his voice husky, "I'm sorry."

She whirled about to face him, her beautiful green eyes filled with tears that couldn't have been caused by fumes from the still-uncut onion. He was dirt. He was pond scum, the lowest of the low. "Aw, Court, please don't cry," he pleaded, her tears ripping at his heart. "I mean it, honey. I was way out of line. I'm really sorry."

Her mouth opened once, twice, before she spoke, and her words figuratively knocked him flat. "*You're* sorry? *You're* sorry? You big dope! It wasn't *your* fault! *I'm* the one who's sorry. *I'm* the loose cannon on this ship. Don't you know that?"

He watched as her bottom lip began to tremble, then pulled her into his arms, to cradle her against his chest. *She's sorry?* he thought, trying to regain his mental balance. He slipped the fingers of one hand through her long black hair, using the other hand to gently pat her back as his mind raced to sort through their argument in an attempt to figure out how *his* oral misstep had become *her* fault.

Her arms, which had tightened convulsively around his waist, began to move, her fingers insinuating themselves between shirt and slacks to trace small circles against his spine.

Courtney wasn't seducing him—or at least he didn't think *she* thought she was seducing him, although it sure felt like seduction to him. She was simply touching, reaching out to reestablish contact with him, and he was glad he was old enough, and mature enough, to understand the difference. Or he hoped he was.

Grimacing, Adam dropped anchor on his libido. He leaned down to kiss the top of her head. "Why don't we call it a draw?" he suggested quietly. "I put one foot in my mouth and you helped shove in the other one. We're even. However, if you don't stop doing that cutesy little thing with your hands we're going to be more than even. We're going to be horizontal, right here, on the kitchen floor, and I don't think that's exactly what you had in mind."

Courtney looked up at him, her eyes still bright, but the threat of tears gone. "No, that wasn't what I had in mind. How did you get so smart?" she asked, quickly removing her fingers and patting his shirt back into place.

"Male intuition," he told her, smoothing back her hair with his hands. "Did you females think you had a patent on it? Now, go wash your face or whatever it is you may want to do while I shove the food back in the refrigerator. We can snack on it later. Right now, Ms. I'm-Courtney-Blackmun-and-you're-not, you and I are going out to dinner."

"Your treat?" she asked, the reappearance of her smile showing him more than anything else that he was beginning to be able to read her correctly at least some of the time.

He shook his head. "We were both wrong. We'll go Dutch," he said, kissing her forehead before turning away to pick up the onion. "Now get a move on— I'm hungry."

He felt her hand on his arm and turned back to face her. She was staring at him strangely, intently. He felt the weight of the onion being removed from his hand as she tossed the vegetable in the general direction of the counter.

He watched, mesmerized, as Courtney moved closer, running her hands slowly up his arms, to link them behind his head. "You're a nice man, Adam Richardson," she said huskily, pulling him down to her. "You're a very nice man, and I think I would like to kiss you. Now, you wonderful Boy-Scout-intent-on-doing-a-good-deed, what are you going to do about *that*?"

Adam was confused. He knew he had been right not to try to seduce her into a better mood. She had even told him so, hadn't she? So how come the sudden about-face? He'd read somewhere that women are turned on by sensitive men. It must be true. It was quite a revelation. Even astounding. And very, very erotic.

He waited, entranced, as the tip of Courtney's tongue slipped out to moisten her lips. The witch! She *was* trying to seduce him. He'd be damned if he could figure it out. But wait a minute. What was he trying to figure out? Where was the problem? Wasn't this just what he had been wanting to happen—hoping would happen—ever since he'd seen her gorgeous long legs step out of the Mercedes and into his life? Why was he trying to complicate things by attempting to assign rational explanations to them? This was not the time for rational explanations.

"Adam," he heard her purr, her hands sliding forward over his shoulders to caress his chest, "are you going to let me kiss you or not?"

He grinned. He knew it was a grin—a wicked, devilish, to-hell-with-it grin. "Be gentle," he warned, lowering his head to hers, until the warm provocative touch of her lips on his chased all the laughter from his mind.

The kiss was explosive, setting off colorful fireworks behind his closed eyelids and igniting a raging forest fire deep in his belly. Courtney felt like a flame in his arms, a molten fire that threatened to consume them both.

He couldn't breathe. He didn't think he even remembered *how* to breathe. For all the kisses they had already shared, for all the moments she had lain in his arms allowing him small liberties like some high-school boy on prom night, this particular kiss made more impact on his senses than anything that had gone before it.

And she was feeling it, too. He was sure of it. Her hands were clutching at him as if she couldn't get close enough to him, couldn't get her fill of him. Her mouth was soft and pliant, her tongue dueling with his as they melded together from chest to thigh.

He didn't know what he would have done, what they would have done, if the phone hadn't rung at that moment, if Sydney hadn't called to tell her mother all about her new school. He didn't know if she would have stopped him, or if he could have stopped what she had so artlessly started.

He only knew that he was drowning and rapidly going down for the third time. The moment Courtney hung up the phone he was waiting with her coat in his hand, and he dragged her out of the condo before she could protest. He knew he would have to put a restaurant table and the company of other people between them until they'd both had time to consider what had almost happened.

He was beautiful as he lay on his back in front of the fire in the night-darkened living room, deeply asleep, his manly features somehow softened so that there was a certain irresistible vulnerability about him.

His lashes were long and as dark as his hair. They even curled. Eyelashes any woman would sell her soul to have.

Courtney's hand moved to lightly push back a lock

of hair that had fallen forward onto his forehead, and she continued her inventory.

His eyebrows were perfect—not too thin, not too bushy, just nice, cleanly sculpted eyebrows that could question and laugh and mirror his every mood.

Even passion. Oh, yes, his eyebrows were eloquent in passion. They had arched slightly in question as his hand had slid slowly upward to capture her breast, had soared like graceful sea gulls as he'd hovered over her, preparing to swoop down and claim her mouth with another of his mind-destroying kisses. They'd dived toward the bridge of his nose like incoming waves about to crash upon the sand as he had pulled her head against his chest and schooled himself to go no farther.

She shifted slightly on the soft carpet, moving more fully onto her side. *The better to see you, my dear,* she thought, stifling a giggle. The soft blue blanket, the one he had drawn up over them before they had drifted off to sleep, was riding low on his hips, so that his slacks were visible. She stared at his bare upper torso, blushing as she remembered divesting him of his shirt, devouring him with her eyes. Yes, he was beautiful.

But it was more than that. This was more than physical attraction. He appealed to her head, her heart. When and if they ever made love, he would love her with his mind, as well as his body, turning the act into a consummate work of art.

Yet they had not made love. Not when she had all but seduced him, and not even when they had returned to her condo after staring at each other across a dinner table while the food they had ordered grew cold.

Adam had only started a fire in the fireplace, and they had shared glasses of wine and another passionate yet unfulfilling interlude on the soft carpet before he had taken her in his arms and fallen asleep.

She continued to stare at him, silently thanking him for his understanding, yet vaguely dissatisfied. Not that she really wanted him to make love to her—that was ridiculous! But couldn't he put up more of a fight? Was it really that easy to kiss her, to hold her—and then *fall asleep*?

Her eyes narrowed as she considered this idea, an idea that left her wondering if, at thirty-three, she was not as attractive as she once had been. She considered this unpalatable idea as she traced Adam's eyebrows with one fingertip, then discarded it. No, Adam didn't act as if she were unattractive.

He was just being a gentleman, allowing their relationship to develop at the pace she was setting.

He was gentle, but strong, the sort of man a woman could lean on and yet not feel dominated by his strength. A man a woman could trust. Her trust in him, and Adam's willingness to allow her to set the tone of their relationship gave Courtney new courage, and she continued her inspection.

Her gaze ran along the line from chin to shoulder. The clean definition of his muscles still surprised her, for he did not look ungraceful in clothing, as many muscular men did. His muscles rippled rather than bulged. Besides, he had a lovely little valley between his shoulder and his rib cage that seemed to have been specially fashioned as a resting place for her head.

Her hand moved to touch that spot, then drifted lower, to trace the line of soft black hair that arrowed downward toward the blanket. His muscles twitched slightly at her light touch, bringing a smile to her lips. Ticklish, was he? If her fingers tickled him, what would her hair do? She flipped her hair so that it all hung down from one side of her head, then raised herself up on one elbow. Leaning over him, facing him, she allowed her hair to glide back and forth across his skin, wondering what his reaction would be.

She didn't have long to wait. Within seconds the gray eyes were open, staring into her green ones. His eyebrows arched slightly; he was questioning her again, silently asking whether or not it was all right to proceed.

"Did—did I wake you?" she asked as she sat up, abruptly aware of what she had been doing while he had lain there in front of her, defenseless. "I'm sorry."

"I'm not," Adam answered, his voice husky as he reached up a hand to lightly stroke her arm. "I don't see why you should be having all the fun."

Courtney knew she was on the brink of what could be the largest step she had taken in her personal life since Rob's death. What did she really want? And how long was Adam going to be content with half measures? Her teeth began to chatter and she reached for the blanket, allowing her hair to swing forward to hide her panicked expression until she could lay her head on his chest.

"Cold?" Adam asked, pulling the cover over her more completely.

"Scared," she answered honestly, her hand slipping around his waist.

"That makes two of us," he said, sighing. "Close your eyes, Courtney, and rest that overactive brain of yours. We can talk when we're not so tired."

Courtney sighed in relief. She could still trust him, even when she couldn't trust herself. "You know what? I could really learn to like you, Chester," she told him, then obediently closed her eyes.

When Courtney awoke again it was after eleven o'clock. She was starving, and she knew that only a full meal of meat and vegetables would satisfy her. Slowly, so as not to wake Adam, she disengaged herself from his embrace and rose from the soft carpet, trying to make out the shapes of the furniture in the darkness.

Away from the dying fire, and without the heat of Adam's body to warm her, she felt suddenly cold. *Cold,* she told herself silently, *not alone. You're having a purely physical reaction to temperature. Emotion has nothing to do with this. Don't start psychoanalyzing yourself or you'll have to put a label on something you don't want to think about—at least not yet.*

It was time to fill her head with ordinary things. For starters, where had she put her shoes? As her eyes became adjusted to the darkness she could make out the outline of her sneakers, and she clutched them to her as she made her way downstairs for a hot shower.

Fifteen minutes later, her hair wrapped turbanlike in a towel, Courtney climbed the spiral staircase to see what she could salvage of the dinner she had begun so many hours earlier. The French fries were a total loss, and she tipped the cookie sheet into the sink and let the soggy potato slices slide into the garbage disposal. The ground beef, however, was another story. Although it was in the microwave, she had never turned the appliance on, so the meat was still only partially thawed.

Reaching into the freezer for the half-empty bag of French fries, Courtney set about making a hefty midnight snack. Cooking was good; cooking was fairly mindless; cooking was something sane and mundane that she could concentrate on—rather than think about what had almost happened in the living room, where Adam lay, still sleeping.

When the tears came, she blamed them on the onion. Onions were notorious for making people cry—everyone knew that. There was nothing unusual about it, nothing to investigate, no hidden meaning behind her tears. Of course there wasn't.

"Oh, damn," Courtney whispered hoarsely, using her navy-blue-sweatshirt-covered forearm to swipe at her stinging eyes. Abandoning the onion, she pressed her hands against the edge of the counter, her head lowered in defeat. "Damn, damn, damn."

"Fumes getting to you?"

Courtney whirled around so violently that the towel fell from her hair to leave her looking, she was sure, like a startled porcupine with all its quills standing at attention. "Why do you always do that?" she demanded, grabbing the towel before it could hit the floor and bending from the waist to quickly wrap it once more around her damp hair. She wasn't ready to see him again. Didn't he know that?

Adam advanced into the room, his shirt tucked back into his slacks but his feet still bare. He looked very much at home in her kitchen. "Why do I always do what?"

She straightened, the towel now firmly back in place, and glared at him. "Sneak up on me, that's what," she answered, turning her back on him to finish chopping the onion. "There are times I think I ought to put a bell on you—like a cat—so that I'll know when you're coming."

He leaned his back against the counter less than a foot away from her, his hands deep in his pockets. "Why is it women always think of collars when they think of men?"

She looked up at him inquisitively. "Meaning?"

Adam shrugged, and she wanted to hit him. "I don't know. Think about it, Court. Men are always complaining that women want to lead them around on a leash—that takes a collar. A ball and chain? Hey, it's just another sort of collar. But a bell, well, that's at least a little different. I will if you will. Then maybe I'll hear you when you try to slip out on me."

Courtney could feel her cheeks redden, and she concentrated her eyes on the job she was doing. If she didn't watch herself, she might just chop off a finger and never even know it. "I woke up and decided I needed a shower and a meal. I didn't sneak out on you, Adam," she said quietly, knowing she was lying and knowing that he knew it, too.

With his hands still in his pockets, he leaned sideways to kiss the back of her neck. "Did so," he teased, his warm breath tickling her nape. Even when she was behaving like a beast with a thorn in her paw, Adam couldn't seem to get enough of her.

And she couldn't get enough of him. That was one of her problems.

Courtney pulled away from his touch, busying herself by making two thick hamburger patties and placing them in the fry pan. "As I've already said, I was hungry, Adam," she explained rationally. "I'm human—it happens."

He used his hands to boost himself up onto the countertop. "You have an answer for everything, Courtney, don't you? It must be wonderful to be so sure of yourself. Tell me, now that we've both had some time to sleep on it—what's your answer about us?"

Courtney felt a shiver run down her spine like icy-cold drops of rain. She had known it had been too good to last. Adam was through being Mr. Nice Guy, and she couldn't really blame him. She turned to look at him as the hamburgers began to sizzle in the pan. "I don't know, Adam," she answered, deliberately hedging. "What's the question?"

He shrugged, and his eyebrows rose slightly. He was questioning again. Questioning her motives. Questioning their relationship. Questioning his place in her life. She could read it in his eyes, in his expression. Courtney fought the urge to turn and run.

"I'm very attracted to you, Courtney," she heard him say, although her eyes were concentrating more on the look of him than the words that came from his mouth. "As a matter of fact, I may even be in danger of falling in love with you."

His eyes were so clear, their expression so heartbreakingly honest, that she felt herself being drawn to them against her will. She picked up the spatula and concentrated on turning over the hamburgers as she responded, she hoped, coolly, "That's not a question, Adam, that's a statement—or a supposition."

He slid off the counter to stand behind her, his hands on her shoulders as she stared at the cooking hamburgers, watching as pink meat juice began to work its way to the surface of each round patty. She felt suddenly ill. Very ill. As a matter of fact, if he didn't take his hands off her she was going to disgrace herself right in front of him! Yet she didn't move. She just stood there, as the hamburgers cooked, waiting for him to speak.

"Courtney?" His voice was low, caressing, debilitating.

She turned off the stove, lifted the hamburgers onto the waiting rolls, then slipped under his hands to stand in front of the sink. "What?" she countered belligerently. "What do you want me to say, Adam. Thank you? All right, thank you. Thank you so very much for sharing that with me. Are you happy now?"

He acknowledged her words with a weak smile.

"Well, at least you didn't add, 'Have a nice day,' like a clerk finishing with a customer." He bowed slightly, formally. "You're welcome, Courtney."

She watched mesmerized, as he took two steps toward her. "Now for the sixty-four-dollar question, Court. How do you feel about me?"

Emotions that had been swirling deep inside Courtney for days suddenly rushed toward the surface to become open for inspection, vulnerable. He may have been fishing, testing the waters with whatever bait he thought would appeal to her, but he couldn't have been prepared to handle the catch that bait brought him. Heaven knew Courtney wasn't prepared for it.

"I loved my husband!" she heard herself explode loudly, her words echoing...pulsating...through the suddenly quiet kitchen. "I *loved* Rob," she whispered hoarsely, one hand to her mouth, her eyes tightly shut as she willed a vision of her dead husband to appear before her mind's eye.

The vision wouldn't materialize. She hadn't been able to summon it on command for several days. All she could see in her mind was Adam.

Adam, bending his head to listen to Sydney's inane teenage chatter.

Adam, walking along the beach, his hands jammed deep in his pants pockets, looking up at the sun.

Adam, lying beside her in front of the fireplace, lightly stroking her cheek as she told him things she had never dared say to anyone else.

Adam...his smile...his gentle eyes...his passionate, giving, taking mouth...

"Courtney?"

She felt his arms go around her, softly propelling her toward a chair in the living room. Even now, through her pain, she silently registered his concern for her. He didn't draw her toward the couch, where he could sit beside her, undermining her strength. He allowed her some much-needed space, as well as the time it would take to compose herself.

"The hamburgers will get cold," she said vaguely, knowing she couldn't eat a single bite.

"Let them," he answered dismissively from the couch. "This is more important." He stopped talking for a moment, time during which she was sure he was gathering his own thoughts, then said, "I know you loved your husband, Court. But, cold as this sounds, life goes on. It has been thirteen years."

She felt her head begin to move slowly back and forth. She was not denying his words. He was right. That wasn't the problem. She tried to explain it to him. "I'm fully aware of that, Adam," she said dully. "Life goes on. It's just…it's just that I feel so guilty."

"Guilty?" Adam repeated like a helpful offstage prompter.

Where are the words? I'm a writer, damn it! Why can't I find the words? She looked across at him, her eyes pleading with him to understand how she felt. "I loved Rob the minute I met him," she said, knowing she was hedging. "I never had anybody, you understand—anybody to love me. He loved me so much."

She took a deep breath. "I've already told you this, Adam. Rob and I hadn't even been married for two years when he died, and I was pregnant for most of the first year and busy with Sydney after that. There was just so little time." She turned away to stare out toward the kitchen. "So little time."

He didn't say anything. He didn't move. He seemed to know, as she knew, that she still hadn't gotten to the point.

She looked at him, not wanting to face him, yet knowing she owed him her complete honesty. "Nobody has touched me since Rob died. I was totally involved with Sydney, then later with my work. There hasn't been the time—nor the inclination. Then I came to Ocean City and met you, and you immediately turned my entire life inside out. I loved Rob, Adam, yet I never was able to talk openly with him about myself the way I've talked with you, telling you things I haven't even told Sydney."

Courtney's voice dropped to a hoarse whisper and she turned away, unable to finish until she was staring at the floor. "I never felt with Rob what I feel when I'm with you—and we haven't even made love. You scare me, Adam Richardson. You scare the hell out of me!"

He was beside her in an instant, kneeling next to the chair. "Courtney," he ordered softly, "look at me." Slowly, reluctantly, she did as he bid. "Now listen to me. You can't compare what we've experienced these past few days with your marriage. You're trying to compare apples with oranges. You were a child—both of you were children. We're adults. We've lived, experienced, wanted, needed, in ways the young Rob and Courtney Blackmun could never have understood. That's life. You can't allow yourself to feel guilty about that."

She hurt for him, she really did. He still didn't understand. She put out her hand, sliding her fingers through the short silky hair above his ear to cup the back of his head. When she spoke her voice was deliberately gentle, as if to soft-pedal the blow her words were sure to deliver. "I can feel guilty, Adam. You see, I want to give you a part of me I never gave Rob—and I don't love you. I can never love you."

The sun was beginning to rise over the ocean as Adam made his way up the beach. He had been out all night, aimlessly walking the streets of Ocean City, which were lit by the yellow vapor lights that illuminated the sidewalk but hid his emotion-ravaged features. As dawn approached he went out onto the beach to walk the long blocks from the boardwalk to the condo.

She didn't love him? *Couldn't* love him? Was she out of her mind? How could she compare a child-bride marriage with their relationship and say that the first was love and the second was merely lust—and *unfulfilled* lust at that? Because that was what she had said. Oh, no, she hadn't actually said it in so many words, but that had been what she'd meant. It had to be. She'd simply refused to put a name to it.

He should have stopped her then—stopped her the moment she'd said she could never love him—and shown her how wrong she was. All he would have had to do was touch her, kiss her, and within moments she would have been his. He had known it. He just hadn't done it.

And with good reason. Courtney had decided that theirs was merely a physical attraction, and if he had succeeded in seducing her he would have only proved her point.

Of course that had been just one of Courtney's arguments. The second, and the most damning, was that she couldn't love him because she couldn't reconcile herself to his supposedly aimless life-style.

"As in you're a worker bee and I'm a drone, living off the work of others?" Adam remembered asking rhetorically as she had stumbled to explain herself. She had looked at him sadly, then nodded.

He stopped to pick up a handful of small stones and toss them one by one into the ocean. *That's* when he should have stopped her. That's when he should have told her the truth. It would have been so easy.

"But, no," he said aloud as he tossed the last stone at the waves, "you didn't do that, did you, big man? You left her there and walked away, never saying a word in your own defense. You let your big mouth dig you a hole the first day you met her and then stubbornly stuck to your lies until that hole was big enough to hop into with both feet!"

He continued his walk, his legs weary, his mind curiously acute in its exhaustion. He knew why he hadn't told her the truth. His reasoning remained the same as it had from the moment he had first begun to believe that Courtney could be the woman he would want to have as his wife. He still wanted her to love him for *who* he was, not *what* he was.

Yes, he wanted her to love him. She *had* to love him, because he now knew he wasn't just in danger of falling in love with her. He loved Courtney Blackmun with all his heart.

Maybe it was asking too much of her, of any woman, but he was going to continue his deception while still trying to win her love. Before he had left her condo he'd made her promise not to run away. He had asked her to give him a chance to prove that what she felt for him was more than a combination of her stressful writer's block, her disappointment with Harry, and one hell of a mutual physical attraction.

"But no more touching—okay?" she had warned before agreeing to his plea. "After all, how else will you ever prove that what we feel for each other isn't purely physical?"

"I hate it when you're right," he had told her as he stood at the open door to the deck, preparing to walk away from her while he still had the will left to carry him. "But remember, Courtney, like MacArthur, I shall return!"

As exit lines went it was a good one, but now he was left with the problem of living up to her condition. How was he supposed to be in the same room with her—on the same planet with her—and not touch her, kiss her, hold her?

And how much time did he have to prove his case? November was rapidly moving into December. With

Sydney in New York, how long was Courtney prepared to remain in Ocean City?

His steps quickened as he neared the condo. He would sleep for a few hours, then give his strategy some thought. This wasn't a football game; this wasn't a campaign. This was his life and, he knew, probably the most important battle he would ever fight.

Chapter Nine

The telephone was ringing as Adam opened the door and he rushed to the kitchen to answer it.

"Adam, is that you breathing heavily on the other end? Maybe I ought to come visit you. I think you've been alone too long, my dear. You're getting kinky."

"And a good, good morning to you, Beatrice," he answered genially, lowering his frame onto the cool tile floor as he held the receiver to his ear. "What's up?"

"Another successful launch of the space shuttle, but then you knew that, didn't you?" she replied in her usual good humor. "Other than that, it's been rather dull around here—leaving me time to think up some fairly farfetched reasons why you haven't phoned. Although it certainly was illuminating to speak with Sydney Blackmun the other day. Such a polite child. Is she still—"

"Sydney?" Adam interrupted, getting to his feet to pace back and forth across the kitchen as far as the extension cord allowed. "She never said anything about— *When* did you hear from her?"

Beatrice's tone seemed purposely noncommittal. "The other day. You had sent her to the condo for frozen pizzas, I believe, just as I was calling to see how you were getting on. Things are certainly changing. I used to give my younger brother a quarter to go to the movies when I wanted to be alone with my boyfriend. Sydney's such a nice well-spoken young person. Ms. Blackmun seems to be doing a fine job of raising her. It's so difficult these days, you know, what with single mothers being forced to be both father and mother to their children and all—"

"What did you tell her?" Adam interrupted quickly as he struggled to remember everything that had happened between that fateful phone call and Sydney's abrupt removal to New York with Suzi Harper. "Does she know who I am?"

"Does she know who you are?" Beatrice repeated. "Who did you tell her you are? I know you wanted to get away from it all for a while, Adam, but it hadn't occurred to me you might take up an alias."

Adam stopped pacing and ran a hand through his hair. "Very funny. I take it you told her—the whole ball of wax," he said in mingled defeat and wry amusement. "How did she take it?"

Beatrice laughed out loud. "She's terribly impressed actually, dear. Who wouldn't be? After all, it's quite an achievement. She didn't tell you she spoke with me? Isn't that strange? I wonder why."

Adam closed his eyes, remembering the rather sly way Sydney had looked at him before leaving with Suzi, as well as her parting words: "See you in the newspapers, Adam." The kid knew, and obviously approved. Fortunately—or unfortunately as it seemed now—Sydney hadn't let her mother in on her little secret. "The little witch," he said under his breath. "She never let on that she knew. No wonder she was so eager to go to New York and leave her mother here with me. Sydney's daddy hunting."

"Adam? Is everything all right? Are you still there? What are you mumbling about? I think I'd better come down to make sure you're all right."

He quickly brought the receiver back to his mouth. "Yes, Beatrice, I'm still here. Yes, everything's fine— at least for the moment—and no, don't come down. Look, I'm sorry I haven't phoned but I've been—"

"Dreadfully busy," Beatrice ended, and Adam could swear he heard the beginnings of an uncharacteristic giggle in her voice. "Yes. Sydney told me all about it. That's why I haven't bothered you. How's it going? Should I be hearing wedding bells anytime soon? I'd do the press releases personally. It would be big news, you know."

"So would murdering my executive assistant. It would make every front page in America," Adam retorted dryly. "Look, Beatrice, I don't want to come down the heavy, and considering the fact that this is *your* condo, would you mind pretending that both it and I don't exist for the next week or so? I've got to—'' Adam was interrupted by the doorbell. "Oh, damn it! Now what? Look, Beatrice, I've got to go. Someone's at the front door. I'll phone you in a week, maybe more, all right?"

The doorbell rang again as Adam hung up the phone over Beatrice's protests about papers he had to sign, and he headed for the stairs, wondering if a reporter had somehow been able to track him down. If one had, Adam would have to get rid of him before Courtney saw him.

He opened the front door slowly, ready to slam it shut if he had been right. He then swung the door wide when he saw the man who stood outside—the man and the long silver chauffeur-driven limousine that was parked in the driveway behind Courtney's Mercedes.

"Sorry to bother you, old man, but there was no answer next door when I rang the bell. I should have realized I might wake you, it being so bloody early and all," the tall exquisitely dressed silver-haired gentleman apologized as he stepped into the foyer uninvited and looked around as if he was interested in purchasing the place. "As it was a depressingly long ride here to see Courtney—we left Manhattan at five or some ungodly hour—I was hoping you might be able to be of some assistance."

Adam gave his head a quick shake, trying to filter through his visitor's words to find the substance—if there was any. "Yes, yes, of course," he answered vaguely, his mind having caught the words "no answer next door" and "to see Courtney."

The man completed his inventory of Beatrice's foyer and looked back at Adam. "My goodness—you're Adam Richardson, aren't you? Of course you are. I never forget a face. First darling Courtney, and now you. I had no idea Ocean City was such a haven for celebrities. It must be the fact that it's in New Jersey that threw me off. I feel quite shabby, having only my villa in Spain—and my house in Puerto Rico, of course, as well as that tiny pied-à-terre in Miami and the family pile in Southampton. I don't count the condo in Manhattan. I shall have to get my agent on the project of finding me a spot here on the beach as soon as possible. You will let me stay here with you until we can locate Courtney, won't you?"

Adam didn't know how he could refuse the man. He considered himself lucky to have gotten a single word in sideways since opening the door. He closed the door and motioned toward the spiral staircase. "Make yourself at home, Mr...."

"Langley," the man ended for him, extending one manicured hand. "Wilbur Langley. I'm Courtney's publisher. You have met Courtney, haven't you? Certainly you have. In a town this deserted I would imagine the two of you are clinging to each other like limpets for companionship. It would be either that or being reduced to sending out messages in bottles with the tide. Really, Adam," he said, settling himself in one of Beatrice's French Provincial chairs, "if I may call you Adam—of course I'd be honored if you called

me Wilbur—it is a lovely little village, if you're re-
cuperating or some such thing.''

Adam walked through to the kitchen to put on some
coffee, offering to share his breakfast with Wilbur.
''Courtney probably just ignored the doorbell, Wilbur.
According to Sydney, she's very good at it—ignoring
unwanted interruptions, that is. Her car is still in the
driveway. Is there any problem?''

Wilbur rose to join Adam, looking as out of place
in the homey room as an English lord lost in the castle
kitchens. ''Lovely place you have here, Adam,'' he
commented, looking around. ''I'm into much this
same period myself at the moment, if I can believe
my latest decorator. A problem, you say? That's what
I'm here to find out. There was this mess about Harry
Gilchrist—she's told you about it, of course? Very
sticky.''

Adam nodded as he whipped four eggs in a glass
bowl. ''Yes, she told me. But I think she's over the
worst of it.''

''Our Courtney is very resilient,'' Wilbur commented, nodding his silver head.

Out of the corner of his eye, Adam watched in
amusement as Wilbur strolled leisurely around the
kitchen, stopped to examine a saltshaker with the
words Ocean City picked out on it in gold paint, then
wandered into the dining room to contemplate a small
extremely unspectacular seascape on the far wall.

How was he going to handle this latest develop-
ment? Nothing was going right. First the news about
Sydney—who could turn up in town at any moment

again like a bad penny—and now Courtney's obviously eccentric publisher showing up big as life to blow his cover. How was he supposed to make Courtney realize she loved him if her condo was going to turn into a meeting place for every Tom, Dick and Wilbur who felt an overwhelming need to see New Jersey in November?

He needed time to think, time to plan, time to convince Courtney that he was worthy of her love. Dividing the scrambled eggs between two plates and putting a piece of buttered toast on each, he carried them into the dining room and motioned for the publisher to take a seat at the table.

"So, Wilbur, you recognized me from my photos in the newspaper, did you?" he commented as he returned to the dining room with two coffee mugs and the coffeepot and sat down. "I didn't realize the New Jersey race got so much attention on the other side of the river. Not only that but, considering the fact that I've been up all night and haven't shaved or changed, I guess that must mean I take a lousy picture."

"On the contrary, dear boy," Wilbur contradicted. "According to my secretary, you're wasting your time in Congress and should be making a fortune in Hollywood." He took a sip of the hot coffee. "Believe me, Adam, the girl should know. The stack of movie magazines she keeps beside her desk is positively depressing. Imagine my distress to have a secretary who doesn't read anything that has no pictures! But with that to one side, may I offer my congratulations? It couldn't have been easy rousting old Jennings. The man has been taking up valuable space in Washington since the French and Indian war.''

Adam smiled modestly, wishing the man weren't so conversant in politics. "I'm just the junior senator, Wilbur," he sidestepped carefully, "and I was merely following in my father's footsteps. His name opened quite a few doors for me along the way."

The publisher waved Adam's protests away. "Nonsense. Humility is wonderful, Senator Richardson, but you're among friends. Your father was a good man, no doubt about it, but you've worked your way up through the ranks. I know, because I've followed your career in the newspapers. Politics is a hobby of mine, you understand."

It would be, Adam thought depressingly. Aloud he corrected kindly, "Senator-*elect,* Wilbur, at least until January. But you're very kind. More coffee?" As he refilled both their cups he racked his brain for some way to explain his situation to the man.

"You're in love with her, of course."

The coffeepot spout collided with Adam's mug with a loud clank. "What—what did you say?" he asked incredulously, looking across the table at the older man, who was sitting at his elegant ease, sipping his coffee.

"I said, you're in love with her. 'Her' being Courtney," Wilbur expanded, leaning forward, a mischievous gleam in his eyes. "I'll confess, Adam. Sydney phoned me the other day at the office and told me everything—not that I wouldn't have recognized you at once when you opened the door to me earlier. You can't imagine my delight! I can only surmise that Courtney's eyes are too clouded by love or she would have guessed your identity. Perhaps she wouldn't have known that you're Senator-elect Richardson, for she has never shared my love of politics, but she certainly would have realized that you are very special.''

Adam propped his elbows on the table and rested his forehead in his hands. *Once Courtney and I are married—if I still have a snowball's chance in hell of that ever taking place—I'll have to remember never to let Sydney within ten feet of a telephone. Well, that puts the cork in it. Courtney will never forgive me—and I don't blame her.* "Courtney doesn't know I'm the junior Senator-elect, Wilbur," he admitted quietly after a moment. "She thinks I'm one of the idle rich. One of the undesirable idle rich, I might add.''

"Yes, Courtney has a working-person's disdain for the purposely idle," Wilbur agreed, nodding his understanding. "Now, let me see. You haven't told her who you are, correct? Yet you're in love with her. I scent an intrigue—or a book plot at the very least. Perhaps I can be of service. Are you nearing 'resolution' or are you still stalled in the 'conflict' of the story? Never mind. I can see the answer in your eyes. Don't ever lie to your constituents, Adam," he advised. "Or play poker.''

Adam told Wilbur everything—at least everything he felt the publisher needed to know—then asked him if he was going to tell Courtney who he was.

"Moi?" Wilbur exclaimed dramatically, pressing one hand to his silk-covered chest. "My dear boy, no.

I am merely an observer. I make it a practice never to interfere. Ask my son-in-law. No—not him. Daniel isn't a good example. Erase him from your mind. But I'll give you another reference—a dozen references—if you wish.''

"There's no need, Wilbur," Adam said, rising to carry the dirty dishes to the kitchen sink. "I'm convinced you'd never do anything to hurt Courtney. She's probably up by now, by the way, while I'm dead on my feet.''

Wilbur came into the kitchen to extend his hand to Adam. "I shall be discretion itself, my new friend," he promised as they shook hands. "And now I shall go have a lovely visit with my favorite author before heading back to New York. I have a meeting with Suzi Harper at three to discuss possible pre-publication quotes concerning one of my author's upcoming releases. I understand you've met our dear Suzi.''

Adam smiled, remembering Courtney's description of Suzi's reputation as a book reviewer. "I've got to ask you, Wilbur. Is Suzi really as intelligent as Courtney says, or was she only being kind?''

The publisher adjusted his French cuffs as he walked toward the staircase. "She's intelligent enough to spot a bad book and articulate enough to rip it to shreds in print," he said, winking at Adam. "But that doesn't worry me, for Langley's never publishes bad books. You will invite me to the wedding, won't you, dear boy? I give lovely presents.''

"Of course," Adam replied, hiding a smile. *Beatrice will take one look at Wilbur and be overwhelmed by the guy, and it'll serve her right,* he thought as he closed the door behind the publisher's custom-made suit.

Courtney waved from the open doorway as Wilbur allowed his chauffeur to help him into the limousine, then turned away before her overly wide smile began to wilt around the edges. What an ordeal! Much as she loved him, Wilbur's effervescent presence had been the last thing she had needed today, when she was feeling so bruised, so vulnerable.

He hadn't pushed her, hadn't even commented on her bleary-eyed puffy-lidded appearance, yet she knew he wasn't unaware of it. Wilbur saw everything; he always had. As a matter of fact, what worried Courtney most at the moment was the fact that Wilbur *hadn't* said anything. It was totally out of character for him.

If there was one bright spot in Wilbur's visit it was his gracious granting of an extension on her contract, "just on the off chance you may wish to extend your vacation in this remote paradise, my dear." *Questions of the Heart* may be moving now, but it was going forward only at a slow crawl and Courtney had accepted the reprieve with thanks.

She walked back to her computer, her footsteps dragging, remembering that Wilbur had told her he'd breakfasted with Adam. Wilbur had also told her that Adam was "a very affable interesting gentleman who scrambled a tolerable egg," but had given her no indication that their conversation may have strayed into

anything remotely personal. It was mind-boggling, for
Courtney was well aware of Wilbur's probing mind
and ability to have people confide their deepest darkest
secrets in him even before the introductions had been
completed.

But Wilbur—who loved intrigue—hadn't given her
any indication that he knew there was anything going
on between her and Adam.

Adam. Courtney's fingers stilled on the keyboard as
she closed her eyes, only to see Adam's face. He was
Elliot, of course. She had admitted that to herself almost from the first, when her writer's block had shattered with that first late-night burst of words. Adam
was the perfect late nineteenth-century hero—handsome, dashing, passionate, independently wealthy and
slightly dangerous.

Yes, Elliot was Adam. But Adam was not Elliot.
He didn't live in a time that demanded no more from
its men than that they wore their clothes well, didn't
eat peas with a knife, were bitingly intelligent and had
all the time in the world to love their women. Adam
had been born into today's world—yet he lived like
the carefree Elliot.

In real life, with rosy romantic notions to one side,
Adam represented everything Courtney, an independent twentieth-century woman, detested. She had
clawed her way to the top through her own hard work.

"Adam Richardson wouldn't know hard work if it
came up and handed him its calling card," she muttered aloud, shutting down the computer as she heard
his familiar knock at the door upstairs. "I can't love

him, and it's only fair to put an end to our relationship once and for all. Then we can both get back to living our lives.''

Courtney's rational resolve lasted all the way up the steps and halfway across the living room, then faltered badly when she saw Adam's face through the glass door. She had only to look at him to call up the smell of him, the taste of him, the heady intoxication his presence in her life had brought her.

Her hands went automatically to her hair, knowing she had passed beyond casual and gone all the way to sloppy. Her face was completely free of makeup and her oversize burgundy sweatshirt, faded too-tight jeans and bare feet weren't exactly a recipe for self-confidence.

Adam, of course, looked fabulous. His clothes, always impeccable, were wrinkle-free and fit him like a second skin. His hair looked freshly washed, his eyes were clear, and his expression was dauntingly sunny. *He probably went straight home last night and slept like a baby,* she thought, her temper flashing quickly as she opened the door a small crack. "I gave at the office," she began, not letting him in.

"You don't even know what I want, Courtney," he pointed out, pushing the door all the way open.

"I know this is a leading question and I'm walking right into a trap by asking it, but, what do you want?"

"You," Adam answered swiftly, adding, "but I won't touch, promise." He stepped past her into the living room and went straight to the closet to get her coat. "Some guy on the radio is forecasting rain for

the next three days, but the sun is shining now. Let's
take advantage of it.''

Courtney folded her arms, sensing that he was about
to bodily push her into her coat. "No can do, grasshopper. This ant has to work," she gritted, deliberately
avoiding his eyes.

"Work, schmerk," Adam scoffed, throwing the
coat over her shoulders and opening the door.
"Whoops—you'll need your sneakers. Don't move—
I know where you usually leave them. You don't need
socks, do you?"

She watched openmouthed as he zipped down the
spiral staircase. Shrugging her arms into the jacket, she
repeated dazedly, "Work, schmerk? He has *got* to be
kidding. What's he trying to prove?"

Adam was back in a flash, sneakers in hand. "Here
you go, Court. Now come on, shake a leg. The sun
waits for no man, you know."

She sat down in a nearby chair, knowing it would
be useless to refuse him. Besides, it might be fun.
"Have you been drinking, Adam?" she asked, reaching for her left sneaker. "Or maybe there's going to
be a full moon tonight. When I talked to Sydney a
little while ago she told me that Suzi is acting
strangely, as well—getting domestic or some such
thing. Suzi—domestic?" She pulled on the other
sneaker. "That's like trying to picture Nancy Reagan
baking brownies." She stood up. "All right, Adam,
let's get this over with."

"You don't have to sound like you're about to walk
the last mile to the electric chair," he said, frowning

in a way that reminded her of a puppy who has brought his master his pipe and slippers and then been kicked for his pains. "You're just going to play a little hooky before the rains come and keep you inside. Trust me in this, Courtney. Having fun isn't that difficult. You might even grow to like it."

"That's what I'm afraid of," Courtney murmured under her breath as she preceded Adam through the door and down the steps to the sand. She had gone only a few steps before he pulled her hand through his arm so that they marched along side by side down the sunny windswept beach.

Adam had been right; a storm definitely was on its way. She could feel its fury building even though the sky was still bright blue. There was something very elemental, something basically satisfying, about walking beside the ocean in this weather, feeling the salty bite of spray on her face, watching the waves crash white and foamy against the stone jetty, and smelling the crisp sea air.

The worries and cares that had seemed so overwhelming just a few minutes ago had been somehow swept from her shoulders by that lovely wind. Courtney smiled, brushing her long hair from her eyes as they walked along, marching in unison like soldiers on parade. "Where are we heading, Sergeant-Major?" she asked above the sound of pounding surf and screaming gulls as she looked up at Adam.

His dark hair was being blown across his forehead, making him look younger and twice as carefree as he had in her living room. "Sergeant-Major? Not me,

Courtney. I'm only a lowly grunt. Did I tell you I was a marine? I was, you know.'' He raised his voice and began to sing. ''From the halls of Montezuma—'''

''—to 'the shores of Gitche Gumee,''' Courtney broke in, then giggled in spite of herself.

'''By the shining Big-Sea-Water, / Stood the wigwam of Nokomis, / Daughter of the Moon, Nokomis,''' Adam completed for her without missing a beat, adding, ''you're a perverted nasty woman, Courtney Blackmun.''

''And you do a nice Longfellow, Adam Richardson,'' she told him, ''for a marine. Did you serve in 'Nam?''

He shook his head. ''I was attached to our embassy in Russia. It gave me a healthy appetite for New Jersey.''

His admission surprised her because it didn't fit her image of him. Just when she thought she could write him off as a wealthy parasite he threw her a curve, and she realized that she really knew very little about him.

As a matter of fact, she knew practically nothing about him. While she had spent whole days and nights telling him things he had no right to know, he had listened sympathetically, and told her very little about himself. Other than the fact that he had been born to wealthy parents and did not work for a living, she knew virtually nothing about him! It was almost as if he wanted her to make up her mind about him without his help.

Now she had learned that he had been a marine. His

face had gotten hard for a moment as he had told her, probably with some memory he wasn't eager to share. Deciding she needed time later by herself to think over what she had just learned, Courtney obliged his unspoken request by changing the subject. "You like Longfellow, Adam?"

"We had to learn *The Song of Hiawatha* in that private school I ran away from a million years ago, but it has stayed with me, so I must like it. The part I like best is: 'As unto the bow the cord is, / So unto the man is woman, / Though she bends him, she obeys him, / Though she draws him, yet she follows, / Useless each without the other!'"

"You couldn't have understand that verse as a child," Courtney said, knowing her voice was shaky. He was reaching her again, worming his way into her heart with his intelligence, his seemingly infinite capacity for finding the way through her protective wall of independence. "It's getting pretty windy, Adam," she suggested in self-defense. "I think we should head back now."

The wind had shifted, so that they were heading directly into the force of the oncoming storm as they made their way back up the beach. Adam's arm came around her waist and she accepted its support gratefully. "Look, Courtney," he said, pointing to the southeast. "The clouds are beginning to boil. Aren't they magnificent?"

She looked at the sky, then up at his face. His gray eyes were sparkling with enthusiasm, his clear tanned skin tautening against his cheekbones as he smiled.

No, she corrected silently, *you're the one who's magnificent, Adam, damn you.*

They were both silent for the length of two blocks, each thinking their own thoughts before Adam spoke again. "You know, Court, this storm reminds me a lot of Sydney."

She looked up at him in question. She should have known there was more to this than a simple walk on the beach. Adam had told her he wasn't going to give up. Now what did he have up his sleeve? *Please, Adam,* she begged silently, *don't ruin this moment.* "Sydney? How? Did she rain on your parade while she was here, Adam?"

He laughed shortly. "Good, Courtney, but off target. No, I was thinking of Sydney herself. I'm crazy about her, but that kid's like a building storm, ready to blow us all down."

Courtney could feel the muscles of her stomach clenching. Yes, he was going to destroy it all by turning serious on her. "I don't know what you're talking about," she denied hotly—too hotly, she knew. "Sydney's perfectly harmless. She's just at that terrible age—all hormones and confusion."

He shook his head, just as she'd known he would. "Sydney's a good kid, a great kid, and she loves you very much. But you confuse her. You say you want what's best for her, yet you won't let her close to the real you. You shouldn't hide things from her anymore, things like your problems with Harry, or your past. She's not a little girl anymore, Court."

Courtney felt the first spitting drops of rain against

her cheeks and was surprised that they didn't hiss into steam from the heat of her anger-flushed features. "Not that it's any of your business—and let me be clear about this, Adam, it is *not* any of your business—but I have my reasons. As a matter of fact I've already told you those reasons."

He stopped on the beach in front of the condo and took hold of Courtney's shoulders. "Yes, Court, you did. You want to protect her. You want her childhood to be happier than yours was. But have you told *her*? She has a right to know."

Courtney raised her hands to lift her hair away from her face—better to glare at Adam, she thought meanly. "You think I'm one of those overprotective mothers, don't you? Do you really think I should have told her that her Uncle Harry was stealing from her mother to finance his gambling addiction? Or is it that you want me to tell Sydney about a past that's dead and gone? Yes, that's it, isn't it? What possible purpose would be served by dredging up all those horror stories about my own deprived childhood? Because that's what you want, isn't it?" She pushed his hands away. "Well, you can just take your suggestions and yourself, Adam Richardson,—*and go straight to hell!*"

She took three steps toward the condo before Adam grabbed her shoulders and swung her around to face him. The rain was coming down harder now and the sunless beach was dark in the midst of the stormy afternoon. She had to blink to keep the rain out of her eyes as she silently pleaded with him to let her go.

She shivered, and it wasn't because she was cold.

This wasn't the same smiling joking Adam of a few minutes earlier. His hair was black with rain, and water streamed down his face and plastered his custom-made clothes against his lean muscular body. He looked so rawly male that for the first time since they had met she was almost afraid of him. His gray eyes were as stormy as the sea as he shouted at her above the noise of wind and rain and pounding surf.

"That's just it, Courtney—the past isn't dead and gone—not for you. Keeping your past from Sydney is just one example. Wake up, for crying out loud! You won't let it go. You're still judging everything on a thirteen-year-old yardstick. You're even judging *me* on that yardstick! You won't let your insecurities go, you won't let Rob go—and it's killing us! Sydney, you, me—us!"

"I don't know what you're talking about!" she shouted back at him, her heart hammering so hard she thought she could hear it above the sound of the storm. She hated him at that moment, hated him because he was right.

His fingers were digging into her shoulders through the fabric of her jacket. "You're getting ready to run again, Courtney. I saw it in your face earlier when you answered the door. I know I promised to go slow, but you're forcing my hand. I love you, Courtney. Did you hear me? Surprise, lady—*I love you!* Damn it, woman, don't blow it. Don't turn your back on our future!"

Before Courtney could think, before she could summon a rebuttal to this unexpected verbal assault, she felt herself being crushed hard against his chest.

Adam's mouth came down to capture hers in a kiss that was half-angry, half-beseeching—and completely devastating.

She clung to him because she had no choice. There was nowhere to go, nowhere to hide, except in the haven of his arms. Her tears mingled with the rain as she returned his kiss, her body responding like a bow to the cord, bending to his passion, to his mastery, to his need.

Chapter Ten

Adam found Courtney in the living room, staring out into the premature darkness as the rain pelted the wooden deck, her arms wrapped tightly around her waist, her slim body encased in a midnight-blue silk bathrobe. Her dark hair was dry now and hung in loose waves on her shoulders. She looked regal and vulnerable at the same time, and his heart ached with love for her.

What they had shared on the rainy windswept beach before she had broken free from him to run to the condo was between them now, both their words and their actions keeping them apart. It had been a wrong move, a fatal move, to try to make her face her past, and he regretted it even as he knew it had been necessary if they were ever to have a future together.

He had followed her into the condo, of course, for she had been too upset for him to feel easy about leaving her alone. He hadn't wanted her to attempt to drive back to New York in the middle of the storm in her need to get away from him.

Adam hadn't known what he expected her to do when she emerged from the bedroom after taking a shower that, to him, had lasted a lifetime. He only knew that he had hurt her and he had to find some way to make her understand that he had done it out of love.

He coughed quietly, alerting her to his presence, and she whirled around, startled, to stare at him. "I made a pot of coffee," he said, handing her a steaming mug before walking over to stand in front of the cold fireplace, giving her room so that she wouldn't think he was going to pounce on her again. "Good night for a fire, isn't it?"

"Thank you, Adam. I'm all out of handy-dandy firelogs," she replied, her smile wan and listless. "You hungry? I could fix something."

"Not me. You?" They were speaking in syllables, not real words, talking about ordinary things instead of what was really on their minds. He took a step toward her. "Court?"

She exploded into action, almost running into the kitchen as she said, "I'm starving, myself, actually. I think I'll make us some eggs."

He followed her into the kitchen to see her standing in front of the open refrigerator door, a carton of eggs in her hand. She wasn't moving. She was simply standing there, staring at the closed freezer door. "Courtney? What's wrong?"

She turned to look at him, her green eyes eloquent with agony. "We don't even like our eggs the same way," she said dully, as if that explained everything. "I like mine over easy and you like yours scrambled. We have nothing in common, Adam. Nothing."

Here it comes, Adam thought, *the farewell scene.* Well, he wasn't surprised. He had known it was coming. It had been just a matter of time. Hell, he had even laid the groundwork for her. "Look, Court—I'm sorry. I had no business telling you how to raise Sydney. Besides, I had an ulterior motive. I was only using Sydney as an example. An example of what's keeping us apart."

She shook her head. "I had a long talk with myself while I was downstairs, and much as I hate to admit it, I think you're right about Sydney. I have been overprotective, shielding her from reality, without ever explaining why. It may even be one of the reasons she's such a handful. I want to thank you for making me see my mistake. But, Adam, that's not what's keeping us apart."

Adam wearily rubbed at his chin, knowing what was coming next. "We're back to the grasshopper-and-the-ant business again, aren't we, Court? Or have we changed to the fried and the scrambled? It's kind of hard keeping up with you."

She replaced the eggs in the refrigerator and closed the door. "I don't know what you mean," she said, leaning back against the counter.

"I mean," he continued quietly, "that you *want* to be in love with me but you detest everything you think

I stand for. Or should I say everything you think I *don't* stand for—such as hard work, suffering and an overriding sense of responsibility. I'm rich, admittedly through no great effort of my own, and it galls the living hell out of you. That's what I mean."

He watched as her eyes turned cold. "Don't try that reverse-snob drivel on me, Chester," she warned tightly. "You may have been born with a silver spoon in your mouth, but I can't hate you for it. No. It's the fact that you *settled* for what you were given and didn't try to do anything with your life that turns my stomach."

"Oh, so I make you sick, do I?" He was beginning to get angry, and his anger goaded him into a stupid statement. "I didn't seem to sicken you a little while ago on the beach, Courtney."

Another woman might have screamed at him; another woman might have cried—or tried to scratch out his eyes. But not Courtney. Oh, no, he thought in grudging admiration, not "I'm Courtney Blackmun." She didn't even blink. "First blood to you, Adam," she complimented calmly, pushing herself away from the counter. "Is it my turn again?"

He pushed a hand through his hair in frustration. "Damn it, Courtney, I'm sorry. That was below the belt, and unworthy of me, no matter how desperate I'm feeling. Go ahead, take your best shot. I deserve it."

She smiled, inclining her head. She was cool, he'd have to give her points for that. Suzi Harper was right—Courtney could certainly be intimidating. "You broke our agreement, Adam," she told him matter-of-factly, adding, "although to be fair I broke it, as well. You promised there would be nothing physical between us again until everything was settled. Obviously that arrangement simply isn't going to work."

"It has only been twenty-four hours, Court," he pointed out, putting on his "trust me" smile deliberately for the first time in or out of the public eye.

"Yes, and given another twenty-four hours we'd break the agreement again. No—" she held out her hand to stop him as he smiled and began to move toward her "—don't do it, Adam, please. There's no future for us. It has to end here."

"Because you don't love me," he said, sure that he couldn't stand hearing those words again from her mouth.

"Love you?" she exploded. "Adam, I don't even *know* you! You're like some dark handsome mystery man who showed up in my life expecting to be taken on faith. I've poured my heart out to you—why, I still don't understand—and you've told me less than nothing about yourself. *Yes*, it has to end. But no," she ended quietly, "you were right yesterday. It has to end because…because I think that I *do* love you."

"I don't believe you, Courtney," he said, turning away, praying that he was at last making the right move. "You see, if you really loved me, I could be a circus clown, or a short-order cook—or even an United States senator. You wouldn't care *what* I was. You'd love me for *who* I was, no matter what was in my past, or what lies ahead in my future. Real love doesn't have conditions. I don't love you because of your past—or in spite of it. I love you because of *who* you are—or who I thought you were. Real love comes from the heart, Courtney, as well as the mind. Think about *that* tomorrow on your drive back to Manhattan.''

Courtney crushed the cigarette in the ashtray in disgust and headed for the bathroom to brush her teeth. The cigarette, and the half dozen she had already smoked, had all tasted terrible, and she found it difficult to understand how she could ever have thought she couldn't live without them.

When she was finished brushing her teeth she packed the brush and paste in a plastic-lined cosmetic bag and carried it into the bedroom, tossing the bag into the open suitcase on the bed.

She had spent a sleepless night—almost a normal occurrence for her since coming to Ocean City—but now dawn was breaking and it was time to go. Closing the suitcase, she walked over to the window to look out into the rain that had fallen without letup since the previous day.

The morning matched her mood—gray, somber, and with no relief in sight.

As she turned away from the window she saw the large pink seashell she had bought for Sydney in a boardwalk gift shop, and she looked around the room for something to wrap it in before packing it. There was something lying on the chair in the corner. It wasn't until she picked it up that she realized it was

Adam's sweater—a cotton navy pullover he had lent her one day when she was cold.

She brought the sweater to her face, rubbing it against her cheek as she breathed in the lingering scent of his after-shave that clung to the soft material. Blinking furiously to hold back tears, she briskly folded the sweater and placed it on top of the bureau to deal with later.

There had already been too many tears shed in this condo, Courtney decided, remembering her two-hour phone conversation with Sydney last night. It had been a difficult phone call and she probably should have waited until she was back in Manhattan to tell Sydney about the years before she was born and the girl's early, unremembered childhood, but now she was glad it was over and the truth was out.

Adam had been right. Sydney hadn't really understood Courtney's relationship with Harry Gilchrist; hadn't understood so many things about her mother that she'd had a right to know.

Courtney sat on the side of the bed, remembering Sydney's confession through the relative anonymity of the phone lines. Sydney had said there had been times she'd believed her mother didn't trust her enough to let her into her life in any way that really mattered. Courtney had been devastated by her daughter's admission.

"How could I have been so blind—so stupid—about my own child?" she wondered aloud in the quiet room. "Adam was right. I have to learn to deal with my past."

Hearing Adam's name spoken in her own voice, Courtney fairly leapt to her feet and rushed to pick up the suitcases and seashell, leaving Adam's sweater behind as she headed for the foyer. It was all there now, her luggage and the heavy canvas cases holding her computer.

She headed upstairs to give those rooms one last check, making sure she was leaving nothing behind. She couldn't wait to get out of Ocean City, back to her daughter and the relationship they could now build together, and away from the man who had been so instrumental in bringing mother and child together on a new, more open, mature level.

But it had to be. There was no other way, no other answer. At least not now. She needed time; time to think, time to come to grips with her past, time to decide if Adam could ever be a part of her future.

Maybe he was right—and she didn't really love him. After all, he had been right about Sydney, about so many things. Or maybe she had been right all along—and what they had shared had been a strong physical attraction that was no real basis for a lasting relationship.

And it wasn't as if he had shared his past with her. He seemed to expect her to take him on faith alone. Could she really love him when she didn't really know who he was? There had to be more to him than she'd seen, yet she had believed herself to be falling in love with what he'd shown her. It was so confusing.

She rubbed at her temples. She wished she hadn't packed the aspirin, for she had a terrible headache. The drive back to Manhattan in the pouring rain was definitely without appeal. Maybe she should wait until the rain stopped. Maybe she should take Adam's sweater back to him. She could tell him about her conversation with Sydney. They could talk about it, maybe even go out for breakfast and—

"A couple more maybes and you'll have an even dozen! You're as crazy as he is, Courtney Blackmun!" she berated herself, pulling on her jacket and picking up her car keys before heading for the stairs. "So he was right about Sydney. Write him a thank-you note. But, for God's sake, don't let yourself believe you can be in the same room with the man without falling under his spell all over again. He may be able to tell himself he has a right to push me about the future, but what future does *he* have? The man exists for today— without a thought for tomorrow. Well, this is one ant who isn't going to stick around for winter to watch the grasshopper freeze his designer jeans-clad buns off!"

He watched through the vertical blinds of the dining room window as Courtney struggled with the case holding her printer, lifting the heavy canvas bag over the lip of the trunk and placing it in the right-hand corner next to the spare tire—the same place it had been when he had unloaded the trunk a lifetime ago.

She was leaving. He wasn't surprised. He would have been surprised if she had stayed.

He lifted the mug to his lips and took a sip of cold coffee, the dregs of the pot he had made at four that morning. Lifting his head, he scratched at the stubble on the underside of his chin, wondering if he should risk shaving. In his present mood he might just slit his throat.

How could he have been so stupid, so stubborn, so mule-headed? Why hadn't he told her the truth? Was he some kind of masochist?

It would have been so simple to say the words that would make the difference. "Courtney," he said now, watching her load the trunk, "I'm not a grasshopper. I only let you think I was because you made such a big deal about the idle rich."

The second black-watch plaid canvas bag slid into the trunk.

"Then, somehow, the whole thing got out of hand and I decided I wanted you to love me for myself, before I told you about the trappings and titles that seem to mean so much to people. Surely you, a famous writer, know what it's like to be courted by people who are impressed by *what* you are."

One by one she loaded the suitcases.

"I've just lived through two years of campaigning and five-hundred-dollar-a-plate rubber-chicken dinners and people fawning all over me because they thought supporting me would help them. I only wanted to be wanted for myself for a change. Stupid of me, huh?"

The trunk lid slammed shut.

"I'm really a magna-cum-laude graduate of two, count 'em, two, colleges, a lawyer, and senator-elect from this great state of New Jersey. I'm an upstanding, productive citizen with a mind, goals, ideals and—hey, look Ma—no cavities. Now—will you marry me?"

Adam let the blinds slide back into place and turned away from the window as Courtney slid behind the wheel of the Mercedes. There was no way he was going to stand there and watch her drive out of his life.

"Nice speech, Richardson," he complimented himself dryly. "And if you had told her any of that—after picking herself up off the floor—she would have killed you for not telling her sooner. Nope, no matter how you slice it, Richardson, you blew it. You're just going to have to wait until Sydney or someone else tells her the truth and hope she'll forgive you—hope she still wants you."

He walked into the living room, picked up his slicker and headed for the door to the deck. Opening the door, he stepped out into the pouring rain, letting the hood slip back over his shoulders as he made his way down to the beach. The rain lashed at him, dripping from his hair onto his face, running coldly down the back of his neck.

He had come to this beach to get away from it all for a while before taking up his position in Washington in January. It had all seemed so simple then; his life had seemed so well-ordered and uncomplicated. He had walked the beach in the sun and wind, and wondered how it would feel to walk it in the rain.

Now he knew. It felt like hell.

Picking up a long thin piece of driftwood as he headed for the flat sand just before the ocean, he tried desperately to recall his first walks on this beach and the peace he had found here, knowing he would never feel that same peace again.

The beach was Courtney's now, and had been since the first time he had seen her here, her arms spread wide as she embraced the singular sensual pleasure of sand and surf and sunlit sky.

Now Courtney was gone and the sun had departed with her. It was time he was gone, as well. There was nothing left for him here. He'd have to pack if he wanted to be back in Basking Ridge before evening.

But first he would walk the beach one last time.

Courtney saw the golden arches and pulled in, suddenly in desperate need of a cup of coffee before heading across the Ninth Street Bridge and off the island.

She sat alone in a corner of the nearly deserted restaurant, her hands hugging the cup for warmth as a chill that had little to do with the weather that invaded her body.

She watched as a young man worked on the grill, turning out unnaturally round eggs that were served on muffins with Canadian bacon and too-yellow cheese. His movements were economical, skilled, and she found herself admiring his expertise.

What was she doing? Was she out of her mind? The man was a short-order cook. Yeah, she thought, so what? Did that make him any less a person? He had a life away from that grill, a life that could include a wife, a child, hopes and dreams. And what if it didn't? What if a short-order cook was all he was, all he wanted to be? Did that make him any less a man?

Was a clown lovable? Of course a clown was lovable. And what was that other thing Adam had mentioned when he was shouting at her? A United States senator, that was it. What hat had he pulled that one out of, for crying out loud? And was a senator more or less lovable than a clown or a cook?

"And who in hell cares?" she heard herself ask, drawing the attention of a plump middle-aged woman who was sweeping the floor near the trash cans. "I love Adam, damn it, and that's all that matters. He can be a beach bum for all I care—just as long as he's *my* loving, caring beach bum! I'm no great prize myself—crying all over his shoulder, dumping my problems in his lap and then hating him for being right."

She dropped the nearly full cup of coffee in the trash can and ran for the Mercedes, fishing the keys from her pocket as she skirted the puddles on the parking lot. A sense of urgency washed over her as she pulled out onto the street. Was it too late? Had he given up on her? Had he gone, leaving her to spend the rest of her life searching for him everywhere she went?

The ride back to the condo was maddening, as if the gods were against her. The rain had subsided to a misting drizzle but that didn't help her as she turned down one dead-end street after another, just as she had done upon her arrival in Ocean City. Mind destroying minutes passed until she found Wesley Avenue and navigated the long beach blocks to the condo.

She pulled into the driveway, exhaling gratefully when she saw the little red sports car still parked on the other side. Her movements clumsy with fear, she raced to his door and rang the bell.

Nothing. There was no answer. Courtney's heart was pounding now. She had to find him. She had to tell him. He had to know that she finally understood what he had meant. He had to know that she loved him—for *who* he was.

"Oh, God," she whispered hoarsely, abandoning her vigil at the door to race around the side of the condo toward the beach. Her sneakers filled with soft wet sand and she nearly lost her balance in her haste to reach a vantage point from which she could see the beach stretch out toward the boardwalk, the direction in which Adam usually took his walks.

The beach was empty. There was nothing—only the raucous screeching of some gulls high above her and the soft slapping sounds of the waves as they kissed the shore. One hand pressed to her mouth to stifle her sobs, Courtney turned toward the boardwalk and began to walk—slowly—because her trembling limbs refused to let her run.

She had only gone a few steps when she saw something out of the corner of her eye. The sand, usually so flat and wet near the ocean, was uneven, as if someone had dragged a stick through it, carving some sort of outsize design into the surface.

She walked closer and saw that the design was a large lopsided heart, with two sets of initials in its center. "'C.D. loves C.B.'" she read aloud, her voice breaking. "Chester Dingman loves Courtney Blackmun. Oh, Adam—my darling Adam! I don't deserve you."

How long she stood staring down at the heart she didn't know, didn't care. Her hair was dripping with rain, her jacket had lost its battle against the elements, and she was wet to the bone. Her torrent of tears had stopped except for a few hiccuping sobs, her teeth were chattering, and her nose was running as it always did when she cried.

But still she stood there, watching as the tide came in to lap eagerly at Adam's creation until it was all gone, until the sand was smooth once more.

Only then did she lift her head and prepare to leave. Turning, she thought she saw someone approaching from farther down the beach. Could it be? *Please, God, let it be Adam.* She wiped at her stinging eyes with the backs of her hands, desperately trying to make out the yellow blur that was moving along close to the water's edge.

Her breath was coming quickly now, as if she had just completed a long race, and she fought the impulse to call out to him, to make him lift his head and see her, to force him into some reaction, some sign that he was willing to accept her as she had finally learned to accept him.

It wasn't until he was within twenty yards of where she stood that he finally looked up to see her. He stopped where he was and held his arms out—to hold her life, her happiness, her future, in front of him— inviting her into his own life.

Laughing…crying…Courtney began to run.

* * *

They were lying on the soft carpet in front of the fireplace in Beatrice's condo, Courtney's head burrowed comfortably against Adam's chest.

"She already knows?"

"Oh, yes. Sydney already knows."

"Who else?"

"Does there have to be a someone else?"

"I don't know. I'm still a little angry with you for allowing me to think poorly of you, when all along you knew that you were anything but a feckless grasshopper. As a matter of fact, I wouldn't turn my back on me if I were you—at least not for a while. Now, who else?"

"Let me think—I'm still trying to sort out all the pronouns in your last sentence. Well, there's your friend Suzi Harper, for one. Sydney's bound to have told her by now. We'll have to watch Sydney once we get to Washington. That kid isn't exactly great at keeping a secret."

"She did a great job of keeping a real doozy from me. And we might have to have a house in Washington, but our real home will be here, in Ocean City, if it's all right with you. You won't be able to keep me away from the beach now that I've discovered it. It's the perfect place for writing—among other things. But let's not change the subject. Who else?"

"Your publisher."

"Wilbur knows, too?" Courtney squeaked in astonishment. "He came down here—and saw me looking like death warmed over—and didn't put me out of my misery? That rat! Who else?"

Adam shrugged, nearly dislodging Courtney's head from that special hollow beneath his shoulder. "I don't know, darling—anybody who bothers to read the occasional newspaper, I'd imagine," he offered facetiously. "My picture has been on the front page a couple of times." He held up his hands as if getting ready to fend off physical attack.

Courtney leaned back on one elbow against the mattress and looked up into his face. "Senator Adam Richardson. It boggles the mind."

"Senator *and Mrs.* Adam Richardson," Adam amended. "I like the sound of that. We'll have to do something about it the minute you finish your book. Is December late enough? I don't think I can wait much longer than that. Of course, now that I think of it, there will probably be times people will call me Mr. Blackmun. I can live with that, too. As long as they don't call me Chester," he added, trying to look stern.

"Of course they won't. *I'm* the only one who will ever call you Chester," Courtney soothed, running her fingers along his bare chest. "And only in bed."

He rolled her over onto her back, taking hold of her hands and pinning them against the carpet. "Because you think I'll make love like the village idiot?" he asked, his lower body moving suggestively against hers.

Courtney closed her eyes for a second, glorying in the feel of his strength against her softness. "I had meant it to be a pet name," she told him, looking up to see his eyebrows soaring high on his forehead. "But, you know," she added consideringly, "now that you mention it..." She let her voice fade away as he rolled over again so that she was lying on top of him. Courtney moaned theatrically, then giggled, her heart more free than it had ever been in her life. "Oh, Chester, what are you going to do now?"

"What am I going to do?" he repeated, leering up at her. "Why, I thought you'd know. I'm going to convince you to make Chester the hero of your next book. Is that all right with you, Mrs. Dingman?"

Courtney smiled, running her fingers through his dark hair. "It's just fine with me, Mr. Dingman. I have only one request. Can we please start my research now?"

Adam Richardson, senator, and Chester Dingham, hero, were more than willing to comply.

* * * * *

Do you want...

Dangerously handsome heroes

Evocative, everlasting love stories

Sizzling and tantalizing sensuality

Incredibly sexy miniseries like **MAN OF THE MONTH**

Red-hot romance

Enticing entertainment that can't be beat!

You'll find all of this, and much *more* each and every month in **SILHOUETTE DESIRE**. Don't miss these unforgettable love stories by some of romance's hottest authors. Silhouette Desire—where your fantasies will always come true....

DES-GEN

WAYS TO *UNEXPECTEDLY* MEET MR. RIGHT:

♡ *Go out with the sexy-sounding stranger your daughter secretly set you up with through a personal ad.*

♡ *RSVP yes to a wedding invitation—soon it might be your turn to say "I do!"*

♡ *Receive a marriage proposal by mail— from a man you've never met.....*

These are just a few of the unexpected ways that written communication leads to love in Silhouette Yours Truly.

Each month, look for two fast-paced, fun and flirtatious Yours Truly novels (with entertaining treats and sneak previews in the back pages) by some of your favorite authors—and some who are sure to become favorites.

YOURS TRULY™:
Love—when you least expect it!

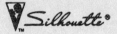

YT-GEN

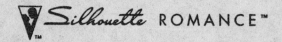
Silhouette ROMANCE™

What's a single dad to do when he needs a wife by next Thursday?

Who's a confirmed bachelor to call when he finds a baby on his doorstep?

How does a plain Jane in love with her gorgeous boss get him to notice her?

From classic love stories to romantic comedies to emotional heart tuggers, **Silhouette Romance** offers six irresistible novels every month by some of your favorite authors! Such as…beloved bestsellers **Diana Palmer, Annette Broadrick, Suzanne Carey, Elizabeth August** and **Marie Ferrarella,** to name just a few—and some sure to become favorites!

Fabulous Fathers…Bundles of Joy…Miniseries… Months of blushing brides and convenient weddings… Holiday celebrations… You'll find all this and much more in **Silhouette Romance**—always emotional, always enjoyable, always about love!

SPECIAL EDITION

Stories of love and life, these powerful novels are tales that you can identify with—romances with "something special" added in!

Fall in love with the stories of authors such as **Nora Roberts, Diana Palmer, Ginna Gray** and many more of your special favorites—as well as wonderful new voices!

Special Edition brings you entertainment for the heart!

SSE-GEN